CRAZY MAN CADE

'Crazy Man Cade' has done it all: foiled a robbery, stopped the beating of an elderly man, halted a kidnapping. But his life is changed forever when an Arapaho brave walks into his camp to tell him that Cade's oldest friend is dying. A perilous journey and a bloody battle ensue and, not being one to settle down, Cade is faced with a choice: will he deny his attraction to one of the Indian girls and ride away from his old friend, and the possibility of a new life?

SPECIAL MESSAGE TO READERS

THE ULVERSCROFT FOUNDATION
(registered UK charity number 264873)
was established in 1972 to provide funds for
research, diagnosis and treatment of eye diseases.
Examples of major projects funded by
the Ulverscroft Foundation are:-

- The Children's Eye Unit at Moorfields Eye Hospital, London
- The Ulverscroft Children's Eye Unit at Great Ormond Street Hospital for Sick Children
- Funding research into eye diseases and treatment at the Department of Ophthalmology, University of Leicester
- The Ulverscroft Vision Research Group, Institute of Child Health
- Twin operating theatres at the Western Ophthalmic Hospital, London
- The Chair of Ophthalmology at the Royal Australian College of Ophthalmologists

You can help further the work of the Foundation
by making a donation or leaving a legacy.
Every contribution is gratefully received. If you
would like to help support the Foundation or
require further information, please contact:

THE ULVERSCROFT FOUNDATION
The Green, Bradgate Road, Anstey
Leicester LE7 7FU, England
Tel: (0116) 236 4325

website: www.foundation.ulverscroft.com

AMOS CARR

---◆---

CRAZY MAN CADE

Complete and Unabridged

LINFORD
Leicester

First published in Great Britain in 2012 by
Robert Hale Limited
London

First Linford Edition
published 2014
by arrangement with
Robert Hale Limited
London

A catalogue record for this book is available
from the British Library.

ISBN 978–1–4448–2028–7

Published by
F. A. Thorpe (Publishing)
Anstey, Leicestershire

Set by Words & Graphics Ltd.
Anstey, Leicestershire
Printed and bound in Great Britain by
T. J. International Ltd., Padstow, Cornwall

This book is printed on acid-free paper

1

The man on the big paint horse rode light and easy in the saddle, reins resting low and loose. He wasn't in any great hurry. The horse loped along with a long, slow, loose stride — there was no urgency. It was going to be a few more days before they reached the town they were headed for.

The rider was relaxed, yet still alert, looking around him, eyes peeled, searching for anything at all that might be out of the ordinary, but they'd had over a week of uneventful riding up to now and there was no reason to suspect that there'd be any sort of trouble to come, so very close to their target. And if there were, he sure as hell could handle most anything that might be thrown at him. Those who knew him, but didn't call him 'friend', and a great many who'd only ever heard of his exploits, called him 'Crazy Man Cade'.

His real name was Jedediah Cade. He'd gotten the handle of 'Crazy Man' due to the fierce, fighting spirit, which was permanently lurking, deep down within his soul, and which reared its ugly head whenever the anger was on him. He carried around inside of him, a ferocity that simmered deep and hot in his veins. The energy of it almost emanated from him, like the heat from the desert. Somehow or other, some people even seemed to be able to feel it, whenever they got close to him, and those folk who felt it, usually gave him a wide berth, even if they had no sort of argument with him.

Cade's name was known far and wide. When he mentioned it anywhere, people's eyes widened at the recognition of it, and the knowledge of what usually followed. Standing at a good six foot four inches and almost as broad, his tautly muscled body was well honed, with not a spare ounce of fat anywhere to be seen. Looking at him, most folk could see he was a force to be reckoned with.

His was an anger that burned long and slow and silent, but could also be mighty quick to explode, given the right situation. He'd carried it deep within him for so long, that he'd learned to feel when the signs began brewing, and, for the most part, he was usually able to control it, to keep it just on the simmer, rather than letting it boil over. For the most part.

He didn't really know where it had all begun, or when. He didn't even want to know. The anger had become a part of his being now, just as much as any other part of him. It surged hotly around his veins, mingling with his blood, and it beat along with the rhythm of his restless heart. It didn't do to get in Cade's way when the anger was upon him. Then, someone would undoubtedly get hurt. It was sometimes Jed Cade, but mostly he was the only one left standing.

His violence was not fuelled by drink,

as it often was with so many other men. It simply burned, deep within him permanently; it belonged with him, as much as his dark chestnut-brown, shoulder-length hair, and deep brown eyes. The anger simmered so close to the surface, that there was always a danger of it erupting at the wrong word, or simply even the wrong glance, in his direction. It just depended how he was feeling on that particular day.

A long, thick, jagged, white scar ran down the length of his left forearm, from elbow to wrist. It was a souvenir of too close an encounter with a tomahawk-wielding Apache. A rogue Apache, who'd been on the wrong end of Cade's famous anger, and had ended up as a dead, and scalped Apache, for his trouble. The scalp was decorating Cade's belt even now.

Those brown eyes of his saw everything, and missed almost nothing, they were as sharp as a cougar's claws. Their gimlet sharpness had served to keep him alive on countless occasions.

He made his living where he could, taking whatever kind of work might come his way, at whatever the time, not caring what side of the law he ended up on, but for the most part staying on the right side of it.

Restlessly moving around from one side of the country to another, and from Mexico to Canada, Jed Cade was unable to settle down in any one place. He seemed to be searching for some indefinable 'thing', which always felt as though it was just out of his reach. His troubled soul could find no rest. His restless heart didn't need it. His head though, well, his head just kept right on telling him that, as he was getting older, he really ought to be thinking about settling down some time soon.

There was no woman, anywhere, though, who had ever yet made him really feel the need to settle. Oh, he'd known many women in his time, a great many. Plenty of whom he'd thought of quite fondly for a little while. But there'd been none with whom he'd ever really contemplated settling down, and making a home.

The nearest he'd ever come to it was one time, way down in Mexico. She was a pretty little filly; name of Juanita Theresa. He visited her regularly, whenever he was in her area. He asked for her by name every time. The things she did for him during those visits made him feel real good, better than most any other woman he'd ever known. She knew just exactly how to please him, and she did it very well. She'd batted her long black lashes at him, to great effect at the time. For more than just a fleeting second, when ever he was with her, his mind began to think about home, a wife, maybe even kids some day.

But after one particularly exciting night with his little lady, she'd gone and spoiled the whole thought, when, come the first creeping pale shafts of the morning sun across the worn out carpet, she sat up in the crumpled, still warm, bed, in the room above the taverna, and held out her hand towards him.

'*That's five dollars, Cade,*' she'd yawned, as she openly, and hungrily, watched him get dressed. He shook his head as he pulled on his boots. What on earth had he been thinking? Sure, good-time girls had gotten wed before now, it wasn't unheard of, but Cade knew that Juanita Theresa was never going to change her ways. He paid her the five dollars. She had been well worth it. But as a wife, well, that wasn't about to happen any time soon, Cade realized. In fact he knew then, that she was never going to be wife material. Her next customer was waiting outside of her door as Jed left. They exchanged glances, nodded, and skirted one another widely.

Maybe, just maybe, one day, there might be another Juanita somewhere for him, but one whom he wouldn't have to pay off after a roll between the sheets. No matter how good it had been.

Cade had been riding the trail for some time now, and today he'd come out onto a wide stage coach trail, one that he knew of old. Some few miles ahead, it landed up at the town of Jemson. He wasn't headed there, but there was a fork in the track a mile or so ahead that would take him on to his actual destination. It'd be about another week or so of riding, but he was in no rush, he had plenty of provisions to last until he got there.

Anyways, he was heartily sick of riding out in the open country right now — it was too hot, too dry and too damn dangerous to be in for long. Pretty soon he'd be down near to the long, thin line of dark, ragged trees that were hanging on close to the river, rolling on from the high mountains. The wide river was heading for the same place he was headed. Thinking about that cool, fresh water, and the dark shade of the trees, he urged the horse onward.

Cade's paint was a breed often derided by whites, as being an Indian horse, because of its colouring. He had large black and white patches across his body, and a thick, black mane and tail, but Cade knew that a coloured horse could blend well into the trees and rocks, it could easily become a ghost in among the shadows. This was a big, strong-boned animal, with powerful quarters and strong shoulders, it would be able to go far, work hard. The horse had turned out to be everything he'd expected of it, and Cade had named him 'Sky'.

As they sauntered along the well-used trail, Cade's sharp ears began to pick up sounds from somewhere up ahead, that just didn't feel quite right out here. Sky's ears were turning back and forth, his nostrils moving and flaring, to try and pick up scents. He too could hear something that was somehow out of the ordinary. Cade moved his legs, and the horse increased his pace, still without any real sense of urgency. Didn't do to go rushing about too much out here unless you really had to.

Glancing around, Cade's attention was attracted by something in the near distance — a thin plume of dust, rising and dispersing into the wide, clear blue sky. He reined Sky in, and stood up high in the stirrups, shading his eyes with his hand, to try and see better just what might lie ahead of them. No buzzards above, so nothing dead for very long yet, if at all. It looked almost like a small camp-fire, but way out here in the middle of a stage coach trail was one hell of a stupid place for a camp-fire.

He set himself back down in the saddle, and with a sharp click of his tongue, urged the paint forward now. He was curious; he needed to see just what was going on. Something up ahead was out of sorts, it was making his spine tingle. He had to find out what it was.

Then, all of a sudden, the unmistake-able, echoing sound of gunshots, rifle fire and men whooping and hollering, told Cade that now was the time he should start rushing. He urged Sky on to a hard gallop, and they headed on up the track. The sounds grew louder as horse and rider grew nearer to the source. Cade's anger began to well up within him. He was ready for a fight.

Cade could see now that a stage was stopped, and a group of men, about four or five of them, were riding around it, shouting, whooping like redskins, and firing into the air. They weren't redskins, though, he could see clearly: they were white men. Riding closer, he could see now that the driver of the stage was slumped over in his seat. To Cade's experienced eye, the man looked well and truly dead. There was an older man, on the floor, leaning against the wheel of the wagon, holding on to his shattered and badly bleeding arm, and Cade could see that there were still passengers in the coach.

As he rode closer, the ragged bunch of men who were shooting and riding around the coach, spotted him. They stopped their yelling and hollering, all of them reining in their prancing, sweating animals, to face towards him. Four of them. OK. Cade smiled crookedly, he sure liked those odds; they stirred up the anger in his belly real good. He eased Sky's speed down to a walk. When he drew close, and all of the men were looking at him, he touched his hand to the brim of his hat. His sharp eyes kept moving all the time, taking in the scene and the men, carefully checking out just who he should target first.

'Howdy, fellers, nice day for it. Mind if I join in with the fun?'

They looked around at one another, they appeared puzzled by his actions. An older man, bone thin, with grey, curling hair, a long drooping moustache, and wearing a red plaid shirt, the obvious leader, pushed his grey a tad closer to Cade, looking him up and down and sneering. He spat on the ground in front of the newcomer.

'What? You wanna *join* us? That's new. Waddya say, boys? Ain't never had no *hombre* ridin' on up askin' for to join us before, huh?' The others laughed nervously with him.

Cade glanced quickly past them into the shade of the coach, where he could glimpse women's bonnets. The anger grew hot within him; women were not fair game, these sons of bitches needed to find that out. Cade ignored the rest of the men, faced up to the leader, and smiled, a cold, hard, angry smile.

The look in his dark eyes quietened the leader for a moment. He shivered, almost crossed himself. Never had he seen such raw evil in a man's eyes before. He knew then that this guy sure meant business. Cade smiled slowly, and calmly shifted in his saddle, moving aside his long leather coat, and exposing his two side arms.

'Now then, let's us just talk about this peaceably, boys, shall we?'

'What's to talk about?' spat one of the gang, a swarthy Mexican-looking guy, sitting on a chestnut gelding that was at least a size too small for him — his feet were almost touching the floor. He indicated Sky with a shift of his greasy head.

'You an Injun then, mister? You're ridin' an Injun horse. No good animals them, only fit for savages to ride, oh yeah, or for cuttin' up and eatin'.' He laughed, a coyote-like sound in the silence now surrounding them.

Cade stifled twin urges then, both to smile at the ridiculous sight of the man on his little horse, and the stronger one, that was bubbling up inside of him at the same time, to kill the arrogant sonofabitch. The man had long, thin black, straggling hair, and a mouth filled with gold teeth. Those teeth glinted in the sunlight, as he leered up at Cade.

'How's about you just ride off out of here, right now, mister, and leave us to our private business, huh, and we might, just, think about letting you live a little while longer.'

'That right?' Cade's eyes were fixed on the leader, still completely, and very obviously, ignoring all of the other men. 'You let your men tell you what happens here then, do you, mister? Or is it *that* guy who's the real leader of this little bunch of no-good sons of whores?' he inclined his head towards Gold Teeth.

The leader's eyes narrowed, and quickly, he turned in his saddle and shot the other man, point blank. Gold Teeth grunted, and grabbed at his chest as he fell in a dead heap at his little horse's feet. The sound of women screaming again, stirred up the hot anger in Cade, and made him itch to wipe the rest of the men out right there and then. Ordinarily, he wouldn't have hesitated for a second, but with the women watching, he knew he had to hold the seething anger at bay for a while longer.

The leader looked angrily around at the other two men, who shuffled uneasily in their saddles, and stared at

15

the ground. He aimed his Colt loosely in their general direction.

'Anybody else want to tell me how to do things huh? Anybody?'

One of them dared to mumble something.

'I think, Boss that — '

'No Jeremiah, you don't think. *You* don't. I'm the one who does all the thinkin' round here. You all just do exactly as I say, or you're gonna end up like Joe there. Savvy?' He was waving his gun around ineffectually.

The other two members of the gang looked down at their dead partner, glanced at one another, then, almost as one man, they turned their horses, and began to ride away, fast. Their horses kicked up the dust, and the men slapped the ends of their reins hard on their animals' necks, in a desperate effort to put as much space between themselves, and their leader, as was possible.

The man in the red plaid shirt blinked: what was going on? They were disobeying him, they'd be made to pay heavy for that later, just as soon as he'd finished off this arrogant guy on the crow-bait Injun horse.

'Hey! You two, you just damn well get back here, you bloody no-good sons of bitches! Get back here! RIGHT NOW!'

A single shot whizzed close past the man's left ear, as he was still shouting at the fast retreating backs of his cronies, and, as he watched in disbelief, one of the fleeing men instantly dropped from his saddle, as if he'd been poleaxed, landing face down in a crumpled heap in the dirt. Before the leader could even turn himself to face Cade, a second shot winged even closer past him, and found its mark right in the centre back of the other outlaw, who hit the ground, and bounced twice, a huge cloud of dust surrounding him.

Their horses, now freed of their burdens, and also of the need to keep running onwards, stopped, turned, and, in the nature of horses everywhere, began to walk back towards the rest of

17

the small 'herd', who were still standing, harnessed to the coach, with the first dead man's mount now standing quietly beside them.

The gang leader turned slowly to face Cade, only to see that two Colts, barrels still smoking, were pointed right at his head.

'Hey! Come on! I thought you wanted to join us, mister!'

He looked wildly around him, as if expecting some help to come from somewhere.

'Join you! Join you? Why, in the name of all that's holy, would I want to do a stupid thing like that? I reckon it'll be you that's joining your *compadres* down in hell any time about now, *muchacho*.'

The man dropped his gun to the floor and leered, coyote-like, at Cade, holding his hands out to his sides, palms upwards.

'See, mister, now I'm unarmed, ain't I, and I can see you ain't the sort that'd be likely to kill an unarmed man now, are you?' He sneered, 'Look, come on, mister, let's just talk about this. I never hurt nobody, did I? Me and the boys was just havin' a bit of horse play is all.'

He attempted a smile again, stretching his lips, so they looked like a slash in his face.

Cade's hard, sharp eyes saw the tiny, almost inconsequential, movement, which, he knew of old, meant that the man was about to reach for another weapon, hidden somewhere on his person. In much less than a split second, Cade had blasted both of his Colts into the red-shirted man, whose dying reflexes kept his hand going for the derringer hidden inside his shirt, even as he fell.

His horse, spooked by the sudden loud noise, started off with a squeal and a jump, the man's leg twisted round as he fell from the saddle, and his boot got caught up in the stirrup. He was dragged along the ground, his bleeding body bouncing, thrashing and turning, like some grotesque puppet, in the dirt and scree, until the horse met up with

19

the other returning animals. It stopped beside them, and they greeted one another, then they all turned and headed back to join the rest, the red-shirted man still being dragged along behind his animal. The small herd reached the other group, stopped, and stood, stamping, and snorting restlessly, with the rest of them at the front of the stage.

Cade slicked his irons back into their cradles, then quickly dismounted, and went to see how best he could help the coach's frightened occupants. His anger was still stirring inside of him, but he was easing it back down now. All the outlaws were dead; he needed to calm himself down, in order to try and calm these people.

There was one elderly, but fairly fit looking, grey-haired, gentleman, whose dark suit had the style of New Orleans about it, and who wasn't wearing a side arm, and a well-dressed, strong-boned, white-haired woman, whom Cade took to be his wife, as they were clinging so tightly on to one another. They looked to be in their sixties or thereabouts. There was also another, similarly outfitted, plump woman, of indeterminate age. Cade reckoned her to be about forty or so.

They were all terrified. The women were crying and trembling, the man was white-faced, and wide-eyed, torn between wanting to run away, and trying to help the women. As Cade appeared at the door of the coach, the women screamed again. The man tried his best to calm and silence them.

'It's OK, ladies. Anna, dear, Mary, calm yourselves, please. This gent has just saved our lives. We'll be fine now. Just fine. How can we thank you, sir?'

He turned to look at Cade, the relief clearly imprinted on his ashen face. The woman who appeared to be his wife, looked up.

'But Frank, what if he's killed them just because he wants to rob us himself?'

'Oh Anna, please think straight, my

21

dear. If he'd wanted that, he'd have killed all of us too by now, wouldn't he?'

'I . . . er . . . well, I guess so, but we heard him say he wanted to join them, what if — '

'I'm sure that was simply a ploy, my dear. After all, the others are gone, and he's made no attempt to harm any of us, has he? Now then, you and Mary stay here, while I go with this gentleman, to see if we can help the driver and his partner.'

Cade stopped him with a hand on his chest, and shook his head. 'No good, sir, driver's gone I'm afraid, and the sidekick's arm's shattered. I reckon a good doc'll have him patched up pretty well, though, and he'll be just fine in a day or two, but we really need to get you folks into town now. I'll go and check that the horses are OK. You're headed for Jemson, yeah?'

The man nodded, and turned back to try and quieten the weeping women again. Cade left Sky range tied, and went over to check the team, six up, all still fastened to the tree, and by that, to the coach. He saw the man leave the coach then, and go to try and help the old man who had been riding shotgun, to his feet.

Checking out the harness animals, Cade could see that they were all fine. He was better with animals than with people anyway, and he ran his hands expertly over their bodies and legs. No injuries or harm to them in any way. They'd still be OK to draw the stage into town from here. He'd tie the outlaws' animals to the back of the vehicle, after he'd bundled the dead men up and thrown them over their saddles. Unfortunately, they had to be taken into town also.

He first went over to the man who'd been dragged by his own horse. It wasn't a pretty sight, best to cover him so the ladies didn't have to see it, so he climbed up on top of the stage and found a tarpaulin. Jumping back down, he wrapped the broken man in it, and

with a grunt of effort, picked him up
and hauled the body up and over one of
the animal's saddles, tying him on
firmly. He went back to the coach then,
and looked in. The women recoiled and
gasped again when he appeared.

'Easy ladies, please, I'm not going to
hurt you, honest,' he held up his hands
to show them he was unarmed. 'I'm
just checking if you're OK is all. Your
man's checkin' out the shotgun rider.
You ain't hurt anywhere, are you?'

The older of the two women sighed
with relief, then leaned forward and
looked him square in the eye.

'Thank you, sir, we are, indeed,
although somewhat shaken, quite fine
otherwise, thanks only to you, Mr . . . ?'

'Cade, ma'am; Jedediah Cade, at
your service, ladies.'

Cade took off his hat so they could
see his face clearly, and smiled at them.
Or what approximated to a smile — he
wasn't used to smiling much, so
doubtless it must have looked like a
snarl to them. They huddled together

again. He turned, and went back to the outlaws, swiftly roping them up, with the lariats from their own animals' saddles, so he could throw them on their horses' backs. They couldn't just leave the men lying out here in the open.

Had he been on his own, Cade might have done just that. No one would have been any the wiser about what had happened out there, but these people would be telling the tale all around Jemson, and the sheriff there would undoubtedly want to have words with him. No need to worry about who'd be paying for their funerals; Gold Teeth had enough in his mouth to pay for the lot of them. Cade thought it best that he should accompany the little party into town, tell his side of the tale, and then get off on his own travels once more. For one thing, the outrider was too badly hurt to drive, and Cade was the only person who could safely get the coach into town right now.

He and the older man then wrapped

the driver in a blanket, and hoisted his body up on to the top of the coach, tying him on, so as to stop the body from falling off, and carefully helped the outrider inside. The ladies strapped the man's injured arm up as best they could, and settled him into a corner as comfortably as was possible. The older man turned to Cade as he left the coach.

'Thank you so very much, Mr Cade, for being here to save my wife and sister and myself. We'd been warned that there might be Injuns along the way, and I guess at first, we sort of thought that these men were Injuns. Hell they were just about as savage as Injuns. Without your help I think we should all undoubtedly have lost our lives anyway, Injuns or not.' He shuddered, looking over his shoulder back at the women, then back to Cade with a grim look on his face. 'And probably much worse than that. My name is Peterson, Frank Peterson, and if I can ever be of any help to you, in any way at all, Mr Cade, you just call on me.'

'Well thank you, sir, but I don't stick around a place for too long, prefer to be on the move, and besides, not all Indians are as nasty as these white bastards were.'

'Never mind, Mr Cade, whenever you happen in this area again, or, most any town where there's a staging post, or telegraph office, I'm well known in most towns hereabouts. If you need any help, of any kind, you just ask for me. I don't go back on my word. We are, all three of us, very deeply in your debt.'

Cade knew from experience, that talk was pretty cheap, the old man would most likely forget him by next week, once they'd told their story all round town until everyone got fed up of hearing it.

'Thank you, sir, I'm much obliged.'

He closed the door, and saluted the man, fastened his horse on to the rear of the coach, with the outlaws' animals, then climbed up into the driving seat. Picking up the reins, he pulled off the brake. Slapping the ribbons, he shouted to the leading animals, 'On boys, ON!'

They all pulled away hard, and the coach set off at a fairly fast pace, kicking up a plume of dust in its wake. They made pretty good time, even though they were slower than they would normally have been, due to the loaded horses they were drawing at the rear.

When they finally reached the town of Jemson, Cade helped the injured man over to the doctor's surgery, then he and the passengers all spent some time in giving their statements to the sheriff. Later, with their thanks, and Peterson's almost sincere promises of help if needed, still ringing far too loudly in his ears, Cade swung back up onto Sky, kicking him into a trot down the main street.

Relieved to be on the move again, they rode on out of town. They headed towards the treeline near the river, to resume their interrupted journey.

2

Cade rode Sky out of the treeline they'd been riding through for the last couple of days, and back down towards the wide river, where he dismounted, stretched out the kinks in his joints, and led the horse down to the water's edge to slake its thirst. They'd been pushing on along the edge of the trees for some time now; they both needed a fresh drink, and a rest for the night.

The river's water was so cold, it made Cade's teeth ache, as he scooped up a handful, and sucked a deep draft of it into his mouth. It had rolled on down from the high mountain range, where their tops were always covered in snow, so that the river that ran closest to them, ran permanently as cold as the thick, blue ice through which it had travelled, and was still almost as cold when it hit the flatter country.

Cade looked up, and around the area, checking it out carefully. His horse had walked further out now, and was almost knee deep in the fast running river. He had his head down low, taking in long, deep drafts of the fresh, bubbling, tumbling water, then shaking his head, snorting the cold water out of his soft nostrils in dazzling, shining droplets, and taking a deep breath, before immersing his nose and mouth back in the freezing water once more.

Cade crouched low at the edge of the river, letting the rushing water flow into, and fill up his canteens, and looking around him carefully. Dark was beginning to fall fast now. He'd bed down hereabouts tonight; it was around another couple of days' ride or so from here to the town he was headed for, but he was in no real rush.

He'd shot a couple of sage hens earlier that day, and his other, dried, provisions would last another couple of days or so. His sharp eyes looked around for a suitable spot to lay out his roll, and set up a small cooking fire. He couldn't sense any danger way out here. He knew there was no chance of any Indian bands coming this way. The nearest ones were at least a good twenty or more miles north.

There was a small green clearing, just between the treeline and the river and not too close to the trees to be uncomfortable. Calling Sky back out of the river, he led him over to the knoll, taking off the saddle and range tying him for the night.

Cade gathered himself some dry branches and kindling for a fire, which didn't take him long to set and light. He soon had a billy of coffee on the go, and plucked and gutted the sage hens, hanging them on a spit above the flames. He threw a handful of beans into a small pan of boiling water on the edge of the fire. Later, with a full belly and the stars beginning to show in the darkening sky, he lay back onto his saddle, hat pushed down over his eyes, hands behind his head, fingers interlocked. He felt real good — warm, full, content, dozy. Life was going pretty fine for him right now.

As the fire died to a golden glow, and the night grew darker and colder, he pulled his blanket around him and settled down. He listened to the night noises and the gentle sounds of the paint fidgeting about in the darkness, munching at the short grass. Cade's eyes began to grow heavy; sleep was closing in on him fast. He reached that infinitesimal moment where the body almost floats, not quite awake, not quite asleep. Then, at almost the same moment that his eyes finally closed, they snapped open again. Instantaneously, almost animal-like, all of his senses were sharply awake and alert.

A sound that didn't belong to the wilderness had jerked his semi-conscious brain back into the moment. Yet, with the most immense self control, tightly honed after many years of living on his wits, instead of immediately leaping up, guns drawn, he continued to lie in the same position, fingers linked behind his head, consciously breathing, evenly, and deeply, so any onlooker would think that he was still asleep. That tiny sound in the night wouldn't have been anywhere near loud enough to have woken a truly sleeping man, so he had to maintain the pretence of sleep.

His eyes shifted over to his right. He could just about make out the large, ghostly shape of the horse close by, its head up, ears pointed towards . . . something, sharp eyes looking towards the treeline. Cade's ears thrummed with the strain of trying to hear what had been responsible for the sudden tiny, insignificant, yet thunderous, sound.

It had been a sound which was almost lost within the night chorus, yet it was one which was definitely not a natural part of that chorus. It was a sound that he knew without any doubt, had been made by a human. Indians? He had felt rested earlier, at ease, about as calm as he ever got, but right now, he could feel the anger beginning to well up inside of him once more. He could almost feel it leaking out of his pores. It moved inside of him, twisting, coiling, growing, waiting to explode free. Something, or more likely, someone, would suffer tonight.

He was growing increasingly restless; the need to go, to leap up and run towards the place where the sound had come from, was gnawing at his insides. He was itching with the desire to move, to go over and kill whoever it was that had been watching him. He could feel the itch, like a nest of fire ants, crawling over his flesh, biting at his skin. It was all he could do to hold himself together, to remain still and wait. Wait, to see just who, or what, had made that inconsequential, yet so very obtrusive, thunderclap of sound.

A casual observer might well have thought he was dead, he was managing to remain so still. But the outer appearance of the man well disguised the immense turmoil he was feeling within. His head was pounding from straining to try and pick up any further sounds. He watched his horse from beneath the brim of his hat. The paint could hear, or even probably see, what was there, as it continued to look towards the trees, ears pricked, and aimed with interest, towards whatever it was that had startled them. If Sky should start to show any sign of being afraid, or worried about what he could see out there, Cade would see it in his stance, and be up in an instant, but his animal remained relaxed, yet alert.

A sudden voice splintered the moment. Cade threw off his blanket, and leaped to his feet, gun cocked and ready in his hand, almost at the same second that he heard the voice, looking towards the treeline, eyes narrowed to try and make out just who might be out there within the deep shadows of the trees.

'I was just wondrin' how long you'se gonna lie there playin possum, Cade.'

The voice was almost sandpaper

rough, deep, and with a slight drawl, that spoke of Texas a long time back. Cade sighed with relief as he recognized the voice, and holstered his Colt.

A darker shadow stepped out of the treeline, a bulky, yet indistinct shape, slowly turning from tree shadow, into man. A rugged and tattered old-timer limped towards him, extending his hand and smiling, showing a mouth full of blackened stumps of teeth. Cade stepped forward, extending his own hand in turn, and met that of the older man. They shook hands warmly, and clasped each other's arms tightly.

'Lordy, Bear, you were almost jerky, you ole fool! You any idea how close you came?'

The older man snorted derisively.

'You ain't fast enough, kid.'

They laughed together and the tension eased fast. Cade threw another couple of hands full of wood on to the still glowing embers of the fire he'd made earlier, and stirred them around until they flared back into life. He pulled the coffee pot over to sit on the flames once more, sat himself down on a log, and motioned his visitor to sit beside him. He looked up at the old man as he headed for the fire.

'What you doin' hereabouts anyways, Bear? Last time I heard, you'd settled down in Mexico with some little *chiquita* half your age! She out here with you?'

Cade looked around theatrically, smiling broadly. Bear spat a wad of chawin' baccy into the fire. It hissed, and spluttered in the hot ashes.

'Be good if it was only half true, eh, Jed? Me, settled down for more'n a few hours? Where in the name of all that's holy, or might be so, did you get that? Tried it once, some time back, couldn't be doin' with stayin' put in one place so long, so lit out again. Anyways, that's almost as stupid as that one I heard about you, that Crazy Man Cade had gone and gotten hisself a wife, and kids, and was running a store in Tampa! Now that really would make you bloody crazy, huh?'

They both laughed out loud, and the night echoed with the sounds. Bear sat himself down on a large boulder, close to his friend, and the two men sat staring at the fire, waiting for the coffee to get back up to temperature.

Bear was just about on the wrong side of seventy, and, despite arthritis in his back and legs, and a permanent limp left over from one of his close encounters, he was still wandering around the wilderness. He was a part of it; he just wouldn't be happy in any other life. He wore his silver hair pulled back into two long thick braids, Indian style, and had it tied through with leather thongs, beads, shells and feathers. His beard was mostly white, stained brown with chewing tobacco, and it too, was long, and pulled into two tight braids, which were decorated with similar ornamentation. A pair of the lightest, twinkling, piercing, blue eyes peered out from under bushy white brows.

His clothes were nearly all made from various animal skins, and he wore soft leather, knee-length, beaded, but dirt-encrusted, moccasin boots, wrapped around with long strips of bear skin. Around his neck hung two or three thongs, threaded up with bear teeth and claws. Two old ammunition belts crossed over his barrel-shaped chest, and he holstered a pair of old Colts. A thick, worn, leather belt wrapped twice around his middle, and in it were tucked a large hunting knife that Cade recognized, and a well-worn skinning knife.

He wore a battered and greasy old black Stetson, which had almost no rim left, and was decorated like the rest of his outfit, along with a bunch of eagle and magpie feathers tucked into the ragged hat band. Over all his clothes, he wore a voluminous, almost floor length, cloak, made of patches of many different kinds of furs, which were crudely stitched together with sinew. All in all, the clothes which he wore served to create a good disguise within the shadows of the trees.

Bear pelts could fetch real good money, but there were not many men about who were courageous, or more likely, foolhardy, enough, to actually go out looking for the creatures. Bear himself was probably just about the only one Cade knew. No one, not even Cade, knew Bear's real name — his escapades had named him long ago. He was about the only man who could really call Jedediah Cade 'friend', even though they only met up together once or twice a year. The two men had first met some six years or so back, and had hit it off almost at once, meeting up with one another whenever, and wherever, their paths happened to cross.

Bear also did some other trapping, mainly beaver, and some prospecting occasionally. He knew, and had long accepted, that one day, one of those bears he was hunting was going to be his last, and that on that fateful day, he'd meet the bear which would take him to his Maker, but until that moment came, he was enjoying his life. The old man was just about as carefree and laid back as Cade was wound up and angry. They complemented one another pretty well, and whenever they did meet, they thoroughly enjoyed one another's company.

On one such previous encounter, Bear had given Cade a present of a huge bear tooth, drilled through, and fastened to a stout leather thong. He said it was from the biggest bear he'd ever seen to date. He'd kept the rest, and gave this one to Cade, who returned the favour by giving the old man a hunting knife he'd bought recently, in the way of the Indian potlatch, trading one gift for another. Bear was more than delighted with the knife, and used it still. Cade treasured the neck thong, and had never taken it off. He almost looked upon Bear as the father he'd lost when he was just a toddler.

'Why didn't you just call out to me,

you stupid old fool?' Cade admonished, 'I was just winding up to come on over there and take off your damn fool scalp!'

'Just checkin' that it really was you and wonderin' how long you could keep up that there possum act of yours. It was a pretty good show, even though I say so myself! Oh, and just so as you know, it'd be me takin' off *your* scalp, kid,' he laughed.

'I could play possum longer than you could keep quiet out there, old man. I reckon as how you're losing your touch. I heard you skulkin' round out there a while back.'

'Only because I was gettin' bored watchin' you pretend to sleep. I had to do somethin' to get your attention, didn't I? Been there since you arrived, watched you makin' your camp. You know, these old joints don't hold with keeping still too long any more — thought you might have heard 'em creakin' way before now. Have to admit the sweet perfume of that meal you were cookin' was makin' my mouth water somethin' awful. I been dribblin' for a while!'

He swiped the back of his gnarled, dirt-encrusted, hand across his mouth, smiling widely at his friend.

'Where's your old mule at, Bear?'

Cade looked around, and handed the old trapper the remains of his meal. Bear began to shovel it down, like it would be his last meal, pausing in mid-chew only to answer Cade's question.

'Oh, old Flash, he died last winter. I got myself two new ones now, left 'em hobbled further back in the trees, I'll go get 'em before we turn in. You still got that damn fool Injun hoss, I see. And he's still goin' barefoot; why's that? You goin' native on us, Cade?'

'Hell, Bear, you know as well as I do, if they go barefoot, riding the trails like we do, goin' up the mountain passes and such, their feet stay in trim naturally, saves the smith's bills. This way there's no danger of him throwin' a shoe way out in the middle of nowhere, and goin' lame on me. Anyway, if'n the worse happens, and I get sent to meet my Maker, then Sky can just clear off and join a herd of brumbies someplace, and not worry about losin' shoes and goin' lame.'

'True enough. Good thinkin', son, morbid, but good. Still think you should get yourself a decent mount, though.' He wiped the grease off his chin with a corner of his cloak.

'What, like those bony old mules you ride? They're only fit for crow bait. Hell no, even the crows wouldn't get a half decent meal off of them. Why don't you get yourself a real horse, Bear? Any kind of horse'd do.'

'Mule's more sure footed, carry more without complainin', less skittish — most of the time. Sure, they can be stubborn as all hell, but ain't nobody, 'specially the Injuns, gonna bother stealin' a mule out from under you.'

The two men swapped insults, yarns and news for a while, until the fire had almost died down once more. Bear had hungrily finished off the remains of the sage hens, and some beans that Cade had left to have for his breakfast, and between them they'd polished off the last of the coffee, then he wandered off into the trees to fetch his pack animals, whilst Cade made another attempt to settle down. Bear unpacked and watered his mules, then hobbled them up close to the paint, setting his bedroll down on the other side of the fire from Cade.

'Y'know, Jed, there's been somethin' eatin' on my mind for a while now.'

'Yeah? Want to talk about it, old man?'

The night was filled with the sounds of hunting birds and small, scurrying creatures, but the men were silent. Cade knew he had to speak, so as to draw the older man out.

'Heck, Bear, y'know, I reckon I must be gettin' almost as old as you, coz these days my mind keeps thinkin', maybe I should settle down some place now.'

'Hell, kid! You. Settle. That'd be the bloody day! You're more of a wanderer than me. But if'n you've been thinkin' that way, well, you best be careful, it's when a man's mind's on such things that he's most off guard, trust me.'

'Yeah well, still gotta meet the right girl don't I? And anyways, who'd want a chewed up loner like me?'

'You'd be surprised. You ain't a bad lookin' kid still. There'd be plenty of girls around ready to take a chance on you, I reckon.'

'Never mind me, what was it you wanted to tell me, then, old man?'

'Nah, no matter, it'll keep. Let's get some sleep.'

Bear turned over, and pulled his tattered blanket up to his chin, conversation over. Cade smiled, knowing he'd get no more out of the stubborn old man this night, and settled back to sleep himself.

The next morning, the two men took their time in breaking their fast with strong coffee and jerky, then carefully packed up their kit, and loaded up their animals. Bear turned round to Cade, as he was tying the pack on one of his mules, twinkling blue eyes suddenly deadly serious.

'You know, Jed, word was you'se wanted in five states.'

'Yeah, well, come on, Bear, we both know that was a couple years or more back. Those times are done now, no one's after me any more — I don't think.' He paused and gazed into space, lost in his thoughts for a moment. 'I was young'n foolish then, old man, young'n foolish. You know what I was like. I'm all growed up now, though,' he added as an afterthought, and smiled across the horse's broad back at his old friend.

'Watch your back, kid, is all I'm saying. You know that wild temper of yours is goin' to land you in some pretty deep shit one of these days. Frankly, I was real surprised to see you were still alive.'

'Hey, I can control my temper all right, old man, I ain't a kid no more.'

47

Bear smiled, as he swung up on to one of his mules.

'That's not what I hear, son. Be seeing you again some time soon, Wakan-Tonka willing.'

Bear touched his hand to his battered hat and rode off slowly, vanishing wraith-like into the trees. Cade mounted up then, and headed off in the opposite direction. He was still heading for Kicking Horse.

3

Kicking Horse was a town that was growing fast. There'd been a gold rush of sorts thereabouts some years back, and the tented village which always came along with the first prospectors, had gradually become a small shanty town, eventually growing and developing into a pretty sizeable settlement.

Houses, stores, drinking and gambling houses and even one or two smarter hotels had been built. Later, it even boasted a proper adobe-built, small, white painted church. It had a stage halt and a telegraph office, and a sheriff had even been elected in recent years. In all, Kicking Horse seemed to be turning into a fairly respectable small town.

But Cade had recently heard on the grapevine, that there was a small group of men who were creating some trouble for the good townsfolk of Kicking Horse, and from what he'd heard, the sheriff was unable to control them.

Or even worse, he was hand in glove with them. Cade had gotten the news when he'd met an old acquaintance who was riding his way on the trail. They'd ridden together for a day or so, and when he gave Cade the news about Kicking Horse, he saw by the look in the other man's brown eyes, that this was just the sort of challenge he would enjoy.

'Watch your back out there, Cade. Those *hombres*, they'll skin you alive soon as look at you. They've got some sort of spread some way outside of town from what I hear, and it's well protected, in a box canyon or something of the like. The chances of getting anywhere near enough to take any of 'em out, are pretty nigh impossible.'

'Oh, you know there's ways, Jake, there's always ways, and I kinda like a challenge, you know that.'

Jake knew better than to ask too

many questions. He knew Cade's anger of old; he'd seen the man when it was on him, and he really didn't want to be on the wrong side of it. He'd seen what happened to those unfortunate men who got on the wrong side of 'Crazy Man' Cade. It wasn't a pretty sight.

Two more nights on the trail, and Kicking Horse was on the horizon. Cade wasn't even sure if the stories that he'd heard about the town were true, nor yet what he'd do about them if they were. He'd check it all out first, then if he found out the stories had been right, he'd make his plans. There was no real rush. First he needed to check into a hotel and settle in.

The first hotel he came to was the Golden Dice, by the look, not the town's best establishment, but fairly clean, and even better, it was cheap. He went in and checked if there was a room, then took the paint over to the livery and bedded him in. The night was uneventful, peaceful almost. Apart from the occasional drunken reveller singing his way home, Cade's sleep was almost undisturbed.

The next morning, he had his breakfast at the hotel and then sauntered around the town. He'd only been to Kicking Horse once before, and that was way back in its early days. The tented village he had seen then had been dirty, full of low-lifers, drunks and plenty of good-time girls. It had been crowded, even downright dangerous. Now, though, it was a fairly clean, and buzzing permanent town, with life, mostly, of a far better kind.

Just out of town, though, the cemetery was crowded, and there was a separate corner which contained a host of simple wooden crosses, in various states of decay. They were for men who'd died without money, and often without names, killed by the lust for the yellow metal, which they had erroneously believed would solve all their problems. The shops that now lined the dirt streets were bright enough; they were obviously doing a pretty good trade. Cade wandered around the place, studying the people walking about. None looked 'wrong'; everyone fitted into their places. Every so often, as he passed them, he thought he saw, in someone's eyes, a look. It was a similar look to the one he'd often seen before, in the eyes of others, who had looked at him in a similar way — fear, guarded eyes, sidling sideways so that they didn't touch him, and hurrying past. It was understandable, he was a comparative stranger here, someone to be wary of, and his size and the overwhelming sense of anger he carried around with him, made it clear he was not a man to be messed with.

Maybe the stories he had heard weren't so shy of the truth after all. Could be there really was someone who was terrorizing these good townsfolk? His hackles rose, the anger churned up inside of him and he had to force himself to calm it down. He knew he needed to keep a level head in order to be of any use hereabouts.

Later that day, when leaving the livery after feeding Sky, Cade stopped, and, glancing around, took stock of the place. Across the main road, way in the back of a side alley, a group of young men were gathered in a huddle. It looked as though they were surrounding someone, a someone who was trying desperately to back away from them. Passers-by, Cade noticed, were skirting around the alley, giving it a wide berth. He had a damned good idea about what was likely to be going on back there. He shoved his hands in his pockets, in an effort to keep the anger under control, and casually sauntered across to the alley.

'Afternoon, boys.'

His eyes took in the small group, and the figure they were terrorizing. They all looked to be about sixteen or so, and they all turned to stare at the newcomer. He could see there was no serious threat to him from any one of them; despite the fact that they were all packing, they were just kids, with no idea about how to look after themselves in a real set to.

A young thug stepped forward from the group, fists clenched tight at his sides, eyeing Cade up and down, lips curling up in a disdainful sneer. He was overweight, his shirt stretched tight over a bulging stomach and a wobbling double chin dripped with sweat. Cade had seen his kind many a time before. Hard, cruel, keeping his small 'gang' in order with threats of violence and torture. That type could never command any sort of real respect from anyone, but thought they had power over people. All they really had was fear hanging around them.

'Who in the hell are you, mister? I ain't never seen you round town before.'

'Name's Cade, Jedediah Cade. I ain't from here. And you, son?'

The youth's eyes flickered — was it in recognition of the name? Or just the thought that here might be someone else he and his gang could terrorize?

Two of the young men behind him carried on pushing and pulling their victim, who was dusty, bloodied and dishevelled, and trying, desperately, but unsuccessfully, to escape their grasp.

Cade could see now that the victim was an older man, well into his sixties. Judging by the look of him, or what Cade could see of him in the shadows of the alley and surrounded by the youths, he was weak, and didn't look well off at all, so why in hell had these young sidewinders picked him out? Because he was too weak to stand up to them all en masse? Or just maybe there was something else going on here. The defiant protagonist took a step towards Cade, fists clenched, chin up, eyes narrowed, no doubt believing he really looked threatening.

'My name ain't no never mind to you, mister, now how's about you just carry right on past, and mind your own. You ain't seen nothin', y'hear?'

The victim in the alley cried out in pain. One of the gang had punched him again and he grunted in his agony, and called out weakly to Cade.

'Help me, please.'

Cade's spine tingled at the weak helplessness in the man's voice. The old man was on his knees in the dirt. Then a pointed boot met his ribs. He grunted and fell backwards. A hard heel stepped onto one of his hands, and ground it into the dirt. Cade heard bones crack even from where he was standing. The man cried out in his agony. Cade tensed, the familiar anger surging, and moving, hot and loud, in his veins, singing in his ears. There were five of them, all swaggering young bucks, trying to find their place in the world, but going the wrong way about it. Somebody was really going to get hurt. But it wouldn't be Cade.

'OK boys, I reckon you've had your fun. Now how's about you let the gent up, and get goin' on your way, huh?'

'Who's gonna make us, old man?'

They all sniggered at that remark. The overweight boy puffed his chest out, and his hand moved a fraction towards the old Colt that he carried. Normally, Cade would have drawn and fired in that split second, without even giving it a moment's thought, but this time, despite the anger within him, he paused. It'd do no good at all to kill this cocksure kid, not in his own town, with witnesses, but the kid and his mates definitely needed to be taught a lesson.

The other four boys were urging their self-appointed leader on. Cade's quick eyes weighed up the gang, and the places they were all standing, he took a couple of steps forward towards the boys, further back into the shadows of the alley. Quickly he glanced down at the victim on the floor; he was awake, groaning quietly, and clawing at his broken hand with his good one.

Then, with the speed of a striking rattler, Cade whipped out both his side arms, and fired four rounds in quick succession, shots that, to an onlooker, would have appeared to be completely random. Two boys suffered painful, but fairly harmless, shoulder grazes — mere flesh wounds — but one was a full-on shoulder shot, knocking the gun out of the hands of the boy who'd drawn his iron when he saw what was happening. The fourth slug sent up a plume of dust right between the feet of the boy who was still standing close to the old man.

Cade purposely didn't go for the leader. Just let the boy watch, that would scare him more than shooting him ever would. Cade's anger grew hotter with each shot. He turned quickly, guns still in his hands. Almost pulled the triggers, but despite his hands shaking with anger, he took tight control. Both of the Colts were aiming straight at the leader now. The boy's eyes widened in alarm and fear when he saw the look in the big man's eyes, and almost immediately he dropped his own gun. The cries that his friends were making, told him it was probably best not to argue any more with this man. He knew he'd gotten off real light.

'Now then, you boys are gonna leave

this gentleman alone right now, and get yourselves off to the doctor to tend to your wounds. You, son,' he used one of his guns to point at their leader, 'you are going to apologize to this gent, and you and me'll take him to the doc to set right the damage you and your pals have done to him.'

Cade eased one gun back into its cradle, and, still covering the boy with the other, he bent to help the older man up, as the other boys disappeared hurriedly. The uninjured one was running hell for leather in one direction, and the other three were each clutching at their various wounds, keen to get as far away as possible from this man, and relieved to have gotten off so lightly, after they'd looked into his eyes, and seen his anger shining fiercely there.

'Right, kid, now, how's about you apologize to the gent first.'

'I-I-I'm sorry, sir', the fat kid was looking at the ground, relieved to have escaped any worse punishment, and probably wondering just what was in store for him.

'Now then, son, you just help this gent up, and get him along to the doc's, and I'll follow you, real close.'

Cade would have expected the sheriff to come running up at the shots. But neither he nor any deputy appeared, and the locals seemed to be taking no notice at all of what was going on. But they kept well away from the young men as they made their way quickly, away from Cade, across the street to the doctor's surgery.

Cade had been in towns like this before, small towns, where the law was allowed to rule, and rode roughshod over the frightened residents. The residents wouldn't want to do anything to get on the wrong side of the so-called law in these towns, and extortion and bullying were the order of the day. Towns like this, and kids like these, did nothing to ease Cade's anger, or the knowledge in him, that he wouldn't feel happy settling down to a life in a place like this.

'You never did give me your name, son,' said Cade, nudging the plump boy in the back with the muzzle of his gun.

'Frank, Frank Lee,' the boy mumbled quickly.

'And yours, mister?'

'My name is George, George Phillips, and I'd like to thank you, sir, for your help in saving me from these little hoodlums. It sure is a good job you were passing when you did.'

'Yeah, but where's the sheriff? He's the one should have really come to your help, him or his deputy.'

'Sheriff Gerrard's headed a posse out of town to hunt down some bank robber. He got a telegraph and lit out yesterday — he left the deputy in charge, Luke Chaney; useless piece of mule shit he is. Probably whooping it up in the whorehouse right about now. Town's usually pretty quiet, just every once in a while there's a rucus like this. Then it seems that the law, or its representatives, are nowhere to be seen.'

The older man gasped as a wave of pain shot through his hand. The boy, Frank, almost fell as the older man stumbled against him. Cade reached out to steady them, keeping his gun lightly touching against Frank's back all the time. When they reached the doctor's office, the two young men with the superficial wounds were leaving, and they stared as the trio entered the surgery, skirting around them, not meeting Cade's cold, brown eyes.

The boy with the bullet in his shoulder was being attended to out back — they could tell by the cries. The three men sat on the hard wooden chairs to wait their turn. The wounded boy eventually staggered out, pale and unsteady, his arm up in a sling. He walked as far over to the opposite side of the small waiting-room, as was humanly possible, eyes fixed on Cade, as if he reckoned that the big man would come right on over and attack him.

Cade made a move, as if to rise, and the boy fell over a chair in his hurry to escape and leave the building. He looked over at his leader as he struggled up from his knees, opened his mouth to speak, and thought better of it, leaving the fallen chair on the floor, and beating a hasty retreat before Cade could do any more damage, real or imagined. Phillips chuckled quietly, as he watched his arrogant attacker running for his life.

'Looks like you've put the fear of God into them today, Mr Cade. Maybe they'll remember this day for a while. I sure do hope so.'

The doctor's assistant came out. 'OK the doctor's ready for the next patient.'

Cade stood, and helped Phillips to his feet. Obediently, Frank stood too. Cade motioned with his head. 'Now, you just get the hell out of here, punk, before I lose my temper again, because next time — well, next time, you won't get off anythin' like so light. The next time it happens, Frank Lee, I'll rip you apart with my bare hands and feed the bloody pieces to the coyotes. Now go, get the hell outa here fast!'

His cold, hard eyes narrowed, and fixed on the fat boy's like a snake on a rabbit, and the boy gulped. This man was dangerous; he knew he'd gotten off real light today. The fat boy left, much faster than Cade had thought he could ever move, and the nurse helped Cade to support George Phillips into the surgery, and sit him on the old leather couch. The doctor looked his new patient over, as the nurse helped him to take off his jacket, waistcoat, shirt and tie, and Cade stood by, watching.

'Well, Mr Phillips, looks like you've really been in the wars today. What on earth's happened to you?'

'Mr Cade here pulled me out of an alley fight, Mac.'

'You've been fighting! In an alley! George Phillips, I'm surprised at you!'

The doctor was amused and incredulous, smiling at his patient, as he swabbed a deep and bleeding cut over the older man's eye. Phillips chuckled.

'No, not me, Mac, some young punks had just decided that I was fair game for a knockabout. I was damned lucky this gent was passing by the alley right about then. It was that young Frank Lee and his gang.'

The doctor nodded, 'Just patched a couple of 'em up — got quite a different story from them, but now it all makes sense,' he smiled.

The nurse, who was handing the equipment to the doctor, looked across at Cade and gave him a quick glance up and down, checking for obvious signs of injuries, a frown creasing her brow. 'Are you hurt too, sir?'

'No, ma'am, I'm fine, thanks for askin'. They were just letting off steam, just kids, none of them any good with an iron anyway.'

'Well, Mr Cade, it's a good job you were passing by that alleyway when you did. Mr Phillips is a very important man hereabouts.'

Cade looked at the older man, who was pretty well patched up by now. He didn't look that important, but then, he had just been knocked about, and stomped on, by a gang of young thugs in a dusty back alley.

'Glad to be of assistance, sir.'

He held out his hand, and the older man shook it firmly.

'Tell you what, Mr Cade, why don't you come on over to our place for dinner tonight, as a way of my sayin' thank you. We're having a few folks from town around.'

'Oh, I don't reckon I'd fit in there, really. I'll be OK back at The Dice, sir. Thanks for the kind offer, though, anyway.'

'Well, look, my daughter will have just got off today's stage. I was headed to meet it when those boys waylaid me. She'll probably have heard what's gone on by now, and I'm sure she'll want to thank you too. She's been away for a few weeks, visiting my old mom, up in Montana. It'd be a great homecoming for her to be able to entertain new guests. Look, please come on over to the staging post with me, and say hello to her at least.'

Phillips dressed, with the nurse's help, then paid the doctor from a thick wad of notes he took from his breast pocket, and headed for the door, a hand on Cade's shoulder almost propelling him forward. Cade wasn't at all comfortable in fancy settings, and it was beginning to sound as if Mr Phillips was somewhat of a big name in town.

'Walk with me, son.' Mr Phillips said, slapping the big man on his shoulder. They both picked up their hats, and left the surgery. 'My daughter, Esme is her name, she'll be waiting for me to pick her up about now and take her home, come with me and say hello.'

Out of politeness, Cade walked alongside the man to the staging post. There were one or two passengers sorting out their luggage, and there, seated on a large, black, travel trunk, was a pretty little blonde, wearing a deep maroon velvet travel outfit, trimmed with thick cream lace. She wore a creamy coloured, high-necked lace blouse, with a bonnet to match the outfit. She was leaning on the handle of a fancy cream parasol. Cade watched her carefully, as he and her father strolled towards her. She was sitting stiffly upright, watching passers-by with a thinly disguised look of disdain on her small, pale face. She was impatient; he watched her tapping her dainty black button-up boots, and drumming her lacy gloved fingers on the handle of the parasol.

'Esme!' Phillips called. She looked around quickly, and jumped up, holding out her arms towards the man.

'Poppa! How are you? Someone said you'd been hurt.'

The two embraced tightly, then Phillips pulled away and held her out at arm's length, looking her up and down adoringly.

'It's nothin'. Esme, you look real fine. That month away did you good, honey.'

'Gran's a lot better now, Poppa. Alice is fine to carry on looking after her — she'll let us know though if she needs me again.'

'Your sister's a good girl, Es, I'm real glad she moved up to Montana to be with her gran. It eases my mind, but I do wish they'd both come back down here now.'

'Poppa, you know Gran wouldn't ever come back here now that Grandpa's gone, she is far too independent.'

Her laugh echoed around them, and Phillips smiled.

'Like all the women in the family, huh Esme, my love!'

The girl looked around, and suddenly noticed Cade standing to the side of them. She looked him up and down disdainfully. For some reason he suddenly felt like a naughty school boy, but he returned her stare, like for like.

'And you are looking at what, may I ask, sir?'

She jutted out her chin as she looked up at him with flashing, angry, eyes. Cade smiled down at her and took off his hat.

'A very pretty, and very sassy, young lady, Miss Phillips.'

He bowed his head towards her.

'Who is this man Poppa? I don't know him. How does he know my name? Will you tell him to go away.'

She turned her back then, very emphatically, on Cade. Phillips smiled up at him.

'Don't you worry, Jed, she's always like this. Esme, this is Mr Cade, be polite to him, he's just saved my life. He rescued me from a gang of young thugs and helped me over to the doctor to get patched up.'

The girl spun round quickly, 'The doctor! Poppa! You're hurt?' She noticed his bandaged hand and gasped. 'Oh, Poppa, I never noticed, I'm so sorry. Of course I should have seen by the dirt all over your clothes, but I never even noticed, I was just so happy to see you again. Does it hurt?' She grabbed his hand, and he winced. His daughter pulled her hands away quickly, 'Sorry, Poppa, oh sorry, sorry!'

Phillips laughed. 'Don't fret, Esme,

I'll be just fine. Thanks to Mr Cade here, I'll live.'

'Well, where's the sheriff got to? He should be here, he should have been the one to save you, Poppa, not this . . . drifter. Where is Gerrard?'

She stamped her foot in petulant anger, quickly looking around the street, and totally ignoring Cade.

'Sheriff Gerrard's out of town, Esme. And Deputy Chaney's off visiting the cats, as usual.'

'Oh well, that's just about typical of this place, leave the civilians to be attacked and hurt, while the so-called lawmen go off enjoying themselves. Montana's far more civilized; maybe I should just have stayed up there!'

She stamped her foot again, hard, and a puff of dust rose around her boot. Cade chuckled quietly.

'What?' she snapped at Cade. 'What's so funny, mister?'

'You are, miss, if you don't mind me sayin' so.'

She spun around to face him full on,

eyes flashing emerald fire up at him.

'Well yes, I do mind you saying so, actually. Why do you find me funny? What a rude man you are. Poppa, will you please just send him away.' She waved her hand casually at him.

'Esme, the man just saved my life, honey, you can't treat him like that. I've just invited him to dinner with us tonight.'

'Poppa, you didn't! Why on earth?' The shock showed clearly on her pale face.

'Esme, listen to me. He — saved — my — life.' Phillips stated pointedly.

She turned and looked Cade up and down slowly, her cold gaze not quite reaching his face, he noticed.

'Yes, well, pay him off, and send him away, like the drifter he is.'

'Esme! You just apologize to Mr Cade, right now!'

'Shan't.' She stamped her foot, and walked off quickly, recognizing her father's waiting buck-board. Phillips watched her flounce off, and sighed.

'You got kids, Mr Cade?'

'Hell no, sir, never had the time, or the inkling to settle down anywhere up to now.'

'Maybe that's a good thing. Kids drive you completely mad at times. Now her momma's passed on, she's become more wild in her ways. I do apologize for my daughter's attitude toward you, Mr Cade. I'll have a good talk to her when we get home. You are still more than welcome to join us for dinner tonight, despite Esme's rudeness.'

He went to pick up his daughter's trunk but Cade beat him to it, knowing that the older man would struggle to lift it with an injured hand, and easily carried it over to the buckboard for him, loading it into the back. The girl stood at the front gazing about, and totally ignored him.

'Thanks again, Mr Cade,' Phillips shook his hand when Cade went back to him, 'Be seein' you tonight?'

'I'll think on it, sir.'

A pronounced huff from the girl made both men smile, as they headed towards the front of the wagon. Esme made to climb up to the seat, lifting her maroon skirt, just high enough to show the white, embroidered, petticoats fluttering daintily around her shiny, black, high-top boots.

Cade realized what would happen as soon as he saw her small foot miss the running board. He moved forward instinctively, and fast. She let out a small cry as she fell, twisting as she went. He was there instantaneously, but wrong footed, and he took the whole weight of her small, but surprisingly muscular, body in his arms, stumbling backwards and tripping over his own feet.

The pair of them ended in an unseemly heap on the wooden sidewalk, beside the buckboard, Esme landing heavily on top of him, her blonde hair tumbling out loose from underneath her bonnet, and covering his face like a blanket.

For what seemed a long, long, moment they lay there. He felt her heart beating fast against his chest, her heat over his body, her breath on his cheek. He could smell her hair, tangled round his face, it smelled sickly sweet, what he supposed French perfume might smell like. Her closeness made him feel a stirring inside that he hadn't felt for some time. He smiled up at her sheepishly.

Blushing prettily, she struggled to extricate herself from the tangle. Cade helped her to her feet, rising to his feet himself, and holding on to her lace gloved hand. Swiftly, and still blushing brightly, the pink of her smooth cheeks clashing jarringly with the maroon of her travelling clothes, she pulled away her hand, brushed her unpinned hair from her eyes angrily, and turned to mount the wagon again.

'Mind if I help you this time, Miss Esme?' smiled Cade.

She huffed again, then paused, and looked down at the floor.

'Very well then, Mr Cade, I do seem to have shaken myself up somewhat.'

She held out her dainty hand to him again. He quickly took hold of it and, taking hold of her elbow with his other hand, helped her to climb up on to her seat.

'Esme! Esme! Are you OK, darling?' Her father was there beside Cade. 'I saw you fall, honey, just couldn't get these aching old bones to move quickly enough to catch you. Thank you Mr Cade, yet again. We are now doubly in your debt.'

Phillips climbed, slowly and painfully up beside his daughter, with a little assistance from Cade, and fussed over his girl like an old mother hen. Then, reassured that she wasn't hurt in any way but her pride, he released the brake and picked up the reins with his good hand. He turned again to his rescuer.

'Please reconsider, Mr Cade, do please come to dinner with us this evening. It's the very least we can do, for all that you have done for us.'

Cade smiled up at Phillips and his girl. She averted her eyes, fussing over her hair, trying to tuck it back into her bonnet, curls shining golden in the sunlight.

'Well, Mr Phillips, I reckon I might just take advantage of your kind offer after all.'

Phillips looked down at Cade, then round at his daughter, and smiled. Slapping the reins, he called back over his shoulder, 'We'll be seeing you about eight, then. Ask anyone around for directions. Till then.'

He waved as they set off. Esme pushed open her parasol quickly. As he watched them go, he felt sure he saw Esme turn, and look back at him beneath the thin fabric of her parasol. But maybe it was just a trick of the light? Then with a shrug, he turned back to go to the hotel and clean himself up. The perfume from her white-blonde hair was still clinging to his face. The memory of her warm heart beating against his chest, widened his smile.

Despite the smile, Cade had an uncomfortable feeling, and not all of it was due to the proximity of Miss Esme Phillips, he was sure. There was definitely something in the air around here, and not just Frank Lee and his little gang of no-goods. A feeling of unrest, of apprehension, of imminent disaster hung over the town like a thunder storm. Cade recognized the feeling — he had known it before and it almost always meant trouble.

Usually this ephemeral feeling was followed by a flare up of his famous anger. When the anger was on him, God help anyone who got on his wrong side. He went into any conflict then like a dervish. It was as if another man had taken over his body, a man over whom he had only tenuous control. He saw red, and exploded, often not even seeming to realize until much later, just what it was that he had done.

Once the anger had subsided, and he looked around him, or someone told him what had occurred, he was often disbelieving of the facts, until he saw the evidence for himself. The anger was like nothing he had ever experienced in any other situation, and he could never explain how it worked. In a strange sort of way, he was sometimes ashamed of himself, for allowing this feeling to take a hold of him in the way it did. He was only alive today though, because he had learned how to control it to a certain extent. When the anger was on him, and he entered into a battle, he did occasionally receive injuries, sometimes quite serious injuries, yet he never felt the pain until much later, when he was being patched up by someone, wherever he'd landed up.

He looked around; one or two people were watching him. They looked away quickly when he glanced their way, carrying on with their daily business, trying to look as if they hadn't seen what had gone on. What *had* gone on?

Cade shook his head, pushed his Stetson back, and walked on. He'd ask at the hotel for the Phillips' address. It was 5.15 p.m. now, plenty of time to clean up before dinner. But what to wear? He'd never before been to a dinner at what seemed to be a pretty high-class establishment. How should he behave? Which knife and fork to use? He knew only too well he was going to feel way out of his depth there. Give him a trail fire, a pot of beans and a billy of coffee any day, over this. But he felt it was the polite thing to be doing.

And Esme Phillips, despite the petulant anger and aloofness, was a pretty little thing — he reckoned he wouldn't mind seeing her again. Nevertheless, he asked the desk clerk for the address of the ranch. The clerk was impressed. The Rocking P was around a half hour's ride out of town. Cade went to his room, cleaned himself up, shaving off his week-old beard, then shook out his cleanest shirt from his pack, spit polished his boots and headed over to pick up his horse.

For once, his anger was at peace, in control. He felt somehow, calm. He'd lived with an anger eating him up for so long, he almost didn't recognize this new feeling. He stopped at the door of the livery and stood for a while, puzzled. Then, shaking his head, he went in and saddled up the paint. They headed out at a steady, loping walk, towards the Rocking P spread.

No need to rush, there was plenty of time to get out there. He had time to think on his way. To think about Esme, her perfume, her golden curls gleaming in the sunlight, her little heart beating so close to his, her hand, small and soft as a bird, nestled in his own. His anger was in check for a while, submerged for now beneath this previously unknown feeling. He rode along, whistling tunelessly, and for once in his life, believed himself to be almost happy.

He found the entrance to the ranch easily enough. It was flanked by two large timber frames supporting the crossbeam, from which the ranch sign hung, creaking gently in the soft evening breeze. Heading in through the gateway, Cade looked around him as he rode. There were a good few head of high class pedigree cattle hanging around, and he could see plenty more off in the distance. It looked a pretty prosperous place.

The house was much larger than most of the other cattle ranches he'd seen, and in very good condition, painted bright white, with black detailing and with no real repairs or work needing doing, a wide veranda ran round the whole of it with a swing and a few chairs dotted around. A small garden, growing a mixture of flowers, and a variety of vegetables, skirted around the house, well tended and obviously watered from the large trough, which was drawing plenty of cool water from a deep borehole in the front yard.

All in all, it was a pretty comfortable looking place. A couple of very good looking horses were already tied at the hitching rail out front. Cade dismounted, and tied up the paint. His hands were sweating with nerves and he wiped them down his jeans as he walked up the steps to the wide front door. He rapped gently, there was no reply, but he could hear music, talking and laughing from inside. He banged a little louder, almost hoping that he wouldn't be heard above the noise. Unfortunately, it wasn't his day.

The door was opened by a slim Spanish woman wearing a white apron, with her thick black hair pulled back into a severe bun in the back of her skull, who looked to be in her late thirties or so. She looked him up and down carefully as she poked her head around the small gap in the door. '*Si?*' her arrogance showed clearly.

He took off his hat. 'Ma'am, Mr Phillips invited me to dinner. Name's Cade. Could you just tell him I'm here, please?'

'*Si.*' She shut the door hard in his face as she disappeared into the house. Cade quickly lifted each leg and wiped his dusty boots down the back of his jeans. Nope, he really shouldn't be here, he was just about to turn around and leave, fast, when the door opened again, and the Spanish girl stood there.

'Mr Phillips, he says you come in, Mr Cade.'

She stepped aside to let him in, looking him up and down as if surveying a tramp. And he supposed that, alongside some of the people here, he did look like a tramp. They all lived hereabouts, had a whole wardrobe of fancy clothes to choose from; he just had a couple of shirts tucked into a saddle-bag. He slowly stepped past her, and stood in the large hall, uncomfortably looking around him, then he took off his Stetson — he knew that was the right thing to do in this sort of society.

'Cade, Jed! Come on in and meet everyone. I didn't think you were going to turn up.'

'Wouldn't miss it for the world, Mr Phillips, sir.'

The slight note of sarcasm in his voice didn't seem to register on

Phillips' ears, as he took Cade's hat and handed it to the girl.

'Put Mr Cade's hat safe in the library with the others, Conchita.'

She took it with extended fingertips and a thinly disguised look of distaste. Phillips led Cade through to a large drawing room, where he could see a group of men and women milling around talking to one another. All obviously knew each other well. Then he spotted Esme. Dressed up in a fancy pale blue satin and lace gown, with pearl earrings and necklace, and with those white-blonde curls piled high on her head, she did look a picture.

She was surrounded by young men, who were all posing and preening, and vying for her attentions. She, in her turn, was fawning and primping, fluttering her eyelashes at all of them. Phillips called across the room, drawing the attention of everyone to him, and making Cade squirm with hot embarrassment.

'Esme! Esme, darling! Here's Mr

86

Cade, he's come to join us after all! Come on, Jed, let's take you over to say hello to her.'

He guided the obviously reluctant Cade across the room, where the group of men around Esme moved aside for them, eyeing Cade up and down suspiciously. Cade's sharp eyes took them all in; he could tell immediately which ones might be threats, and who might be just a tad more friendly towards him. Phillips spoke to him.

'This little soirée is to welcome my Esme home, Jed. She's been away about a month or so now, so I thought we'd have a small dinner in honour of her return. Her mother would have really enjoyed it.'

His face changed and darkened and Cade thought he saw a trace of tears filling the older man's eyes.

'Poppa, don't. Please. You and Conchita were really wonderful to arrange this evening for me, it's truly lovely. Please don't dwell on Momma tonight — I don't want you to be sad.

She's been gone for nigh on five years now, and we do still miss her, but we have to carry on, don't we?'

She squeezed her father's arm, and smiled up at him. He smiled down at her in return, and his face lightened again.

'Esme, darling, say hello to Mr Cade again.'

She held out her hand. He took it awkwardly, and shook it gently, and heard shuffling, quiet murmuring, and a slight, quickly stifled giggle from behind him.

'Hello again, Mr Cade. Thank you for your help today, and for attending here tonight, now please, will you excuse me.'

She withdrew her hand quickly, and immediately turned her back on him, to carry on talking to the other young men. He knew when he'd been dismissed. Maybe he should have kissed her hand, he'd seen it done, but didn't know if this was the right thing to do with a young lady of Esme Phillips' standing. Nor if he should kiss the hand of a young lady to whom he had only just been introduced. Maybe that was why someone was laughing quietly. He'd done it wrong. He was uncomfortable. He knew it had been a mistake to come tonight. And dinner was going be an even bigger embarrassment. Her father put his arm around Cade's shoulders and steered him away from Esme and her admirers.

'Don't worry 'bout her, Jed. Come with me, we'll have a cigar before dinner, eh?'

Phillips had obviously seen how uncomfortable Cade was, and was trying to ease that discomfort. Cade had already decided he was going to leave well before the meal.

'I don't reckon I'll be hangin' around for too long now, Mr Phillips. I feel, well, sorta awkward, you know, in this here kind of company. Thanks for invitin' me over, though. I do appreciate it.'

'Nonsense. If it's the meal you're

worried about, all those knives and forks and such, just you watch me, Jed, follow my lead. I'll make sure you're OK.'

Cade didn't doubt the older man's word, but felt that sitting at their large table, being guided through a meal like a child, and having to make small talk with folk who obviously looked on him with undisguised disdain, was going to be just too much to take. He'd never been in this sort of company before, and was feeling damned uncomfortable. Give him the mountains, or even the desert, with its Gila monsters, scorpions, and rattlers any day. Somehow he figured, even they would be more pleasant company than the men now swarming around Esme.

He followed Phillips into what was obviously his library. Cade could read some, but never, in all his days, had he seen so many books all gathered together in one place. He looked around in awe at the heavy Spanish furniture, a huge and ornate leather-topped desk piled high with paperwork, and the walls filled with shelves of books of all shapes, sizes, and colours, some of which even had what looked like foreign languages printed on their leather spines. He knew then, for a certainty, that he really wouldn't ever fit into this kind of company.

He shared a good cheroot with Phillips nonetheless, sitting in one of the carved and padded, leather upholstered chairs, surrounded by books from all over the known world, and just felt completely uncomfortable, like there was a whole nest of termites in his pants, all chawin' away at his nether regions. He was itching to get out of there as fast as was politely comfortable.

The two men made small talk, mostly centred around Esme, until the dinner gong sounded loudly. Phillips stood up slowly, the beating he'd taken earlier was obviously taking its toll on his body now.

'Come then, Mr Cade, join me,' said Phillips, holding out his hand to guide him forward. Cade stepped to one side, and saw his hat on a pile of others on the couch. He picked it up, and started screwing up the brim in his sweating hands. As they left the library, Cade held out his hand to the older man.

'Well Mr Phillips, it's been real nice. Sorry I won't be stayin' but, well, I guess you can tell, this just ain't my sort of soirée, so I'll be sloping off now. Thanks for the invite. I appreciate it. I wish you and your daughter real well.'

'Well, if you're sure? I know Esme took something of a shine to you — it'd be good for her to see you in there, but I guess I do understand your reluctance. Thanks to you again, from us both, Mr Cade.'

Somehow Cade suspected that Phillips really didn't know his daughter as well as he thought he did. She hadn't taken any sort of a shine to him at all, she simply hated him, for some reason. Never mind, now at least she would be spared having to look at him over the meal. He headed for the door, closely followed by Phillips. As they reached it, someone rapped loudly on it.

'It's OK, Conchita, I'll answer it,' Phillips called, as he opened the door.

Cade saw the badge before he saw the man. It was the elusive sheriff. Why had Phillips invited him? He didn't have a kind word to say about him earlier. The sheriff was a tall skinny man, middle aged, with dark, greasy, slicked-back hair, and a drooping black moustache. He wore a very wide brimmed hat, and a pair of pearl-handled Colts hung low at his sides. As the door was opened, he took off his hat. His eyes were pale, cruel and hard. Cade had met his kind many times before and knew he was big trouble.

'Sheriff, welcome. This here's Mr Cade. He's the one who saved me from Frank Lee and his pals today. Cade, this is Sheriff Gerrard. Mr Cade's just leavin', Sheriff, got some business to attend to.'

Cade and Phillips exchanged a glance; Cade was grateful to Phillips for the cover-up. The sheriff and Cade shook hands stiffly; Gerrard looked Cade up and down, examining him closely.

'Business, eh? Yeah. Well, don't let me stop you. Mr Cade. Now then, let's go say welcome back to your little girl, eh, Phillips?'

He let go of Cade's hand abruptly, and brushed past him without another word.

'Sorry 'bout that, Jed. He's real sweet on Esme, can't wait to get to her, but then, there's a lot of men here-abouts who're sweet on Esme. She seems to enjoy playing them off one another. My little girl's a real heartbreaker. One day, somebody's going to get hurt.'

There was pain in his eyes as he looked down at the floor momentarily. Almost as quickly, he was smiling back up at Cade and shaking his hand.

'You're very welcome here any time, Mr Cade, please, do remember that. And don't forget, if I can ever be of help to you, in any way at all, just call on me.'

Cade knew that this was one man who really meant what he said. They shook hands, and said their goodbyes. Cade mounted Sky with a huge sigh of relief; he'd never fit into that sort of society, it would stifle him in days. They rode off, the sounds of laughter and chatter echoing in the darkness behind him. He slapped the hard-muscled neck of the big paint.

'Well, Sky, old feller, reckon we're better off away from there, huh? Not our type of place — too high falutin' for us, don't you think?' The horse shook its head and snorted loudly. Cade laughed. 'Yeah, that's what I thought.'

He urged Sky onwards, back towards the town, thankful to be away from the place. He'd gotten rid of the termites in his pants now, and just for the hell of it, he urged the paint into the fastest gallop he'd had in a long while, just to feel the wind on his face, blowing away the suffocation of the Phillips house.

Sure, Esme Phillips was a pretty little thing, but she was most definitely not his type, far too up herself for his liking. Well, let some other poor unsuspecting schmuck take her on. Cade would soon be heading off back into the wild, where he really belonged.

4

A couple of days after the soirée at the Phillips house, Cade was sitting outside the general store, minding his business, gathering information, and watching the town folks coming and going; you could learn a lot about folks by just watching them quietly. And he needed to learn whatever he could about this town right now.

'Mr Cade! Mr Cade! Jed!'

A loud and anxious sounding cry alerted him and he turned around to see George Phillips heading towards him as fast as he could, his face grave and white. Cade stood up, and waited for the obviously agitated man to reach him.

'Mr Phillips, you OK, sir? What's happened?'

'No, Mr Cade, I'm so glad you're still in town, I need your help. That useless goddamn sheriff's out of town again, and the deputy's damn well rolling drunk as usual. You're the only man I know I can turn to now.'

'What is it?' Cade asked the breathless man.

'It's Esme. She's gone, Jed! They've taken my Esme!'

Cade felt a hard, cold, fist squeeze his heart. This was the reason he was here in the town.

'Taken her? Where? Who's taken her? How'd you know she's been taken? Sit down here, tell me what you know.'

They sat back down on the bench in front of the general store, across the street from the sheriff's office. Cade tried to talk calmly to the older man, but inside he could feel the beginning of those familiar angry stirrings. Phillips sat heavily, took off his hat, mopped his brow with his kerchief, and pushed his hands back through his greying hair, sighing deeply and shaking his head.

'I just don't know, Mr Cade. I don't know, not really.'

'You don't know what? OK now, you're upset. We'll take it one piece at a time then. How do you know your daughter's actually gone? And how would you know she hasn't just gone for a jaunt? Maybe she'll be back soon — she might be home even now.'

He tried to lighten the other man's spirits.

'No! Her horse has gone, and Conchita said she saw her riding out fast, with two pretty rough looking men. She wouldn't do that of her own accord.'

'You're absolutely sure?'

'Mr Cade! What sort of a girl do you think Esme is!' He was real angry now, and stood to leave. 'She'd no more ride out with two strange men than — than — fly!'

'No, no, of course, I apologize Mr Phillips, I do, but we really do need to try and think of every eventuality. She wasn't, well, 'seeing' any guy that you didn't approve of by any chance?'

Phillips sat back down with a groan

that came from his heart.

'No! Since her momma passed away, Esme and I have got real close, and she talks to Conchita, you remember, our house girl? They're real friendly now and she'd have told her if that was the case. Conchita says it looked like Esme was struggling against one of the men, and the other was leading her horse. She doesn't need a leader, she's a perfectly good rider. And none of her clothes or effects are gone, Conchita checked thoroughly.'

'Any ideas who might be responsible, Mr Phillips? Could it have been one of the men from your party the other night?'

'No, I don't think it could be, no, Conchita said she didn't recognize either of them. But you know Frank Lee and his little bunch are out to get me. Maybe they decided to do it this way. Oh God! What'll they do to her, Cade?'

The look of sheer despair in his eyes hit right to Cade's heart; he knew that he had to do whatever it took. He didn't reply to what was, after all, a rhetorical question. Both men had a good idea of the answer to that one.

'I'll find Miss Esme for you, sir, don't you worry. By God, I *will* find her, and the men who took her will be made to pay for it. Big time. Which way were they headed?'

Cade's anger was singing inside of him, he could feel the familiar churning in his soul.

'Conchita said they rode west from our place, out towards Mile High Bluff. Know it?'

'Nope, but I'll sure as hell find it. You get on back home, sir, just in case she manages to find her way back. I'll go find her.'

'But won't you need to round up some men to help?'

'Nope. I work far better, and faster, alone, sir. Besides, well . . . I've got my own particular way of working, that others might just not agree with.'

'I really don't care what you have to

do, Cade, or how in the hell you do it. Just you get my Esme back for me any way you can, and please, call me George.'

The older man held out his hand and Cade grasped it. He looked into Phillips' tear-filled eyes, and saw the deep and dreadful fear lying there.

'I'll grab my horse and head out right now, George. Which way is it from here?'

Phillips gathered himself, looked around and got his bearings.

'South from here Cade, south. Please, be fast.'

Cade squeezed the man's hand, touched the brim of his hat in salute and hurried off over to the livery. Without bothering to stop and saddle up, he practically threw a rope halter over the head of Sky, and they exploded from the stall, Cade leaping onto his horse's back as they went. He rode faster without a saddle, and right now, he needed speed. Sky was well trained; he'd respond to the halter and Cade's leg commands, and he too seemed to sense the need for urgency.

They pushed on fast for some time. Cade was easily able to follow the tracks of the six shod horses in the dirt; the two who'd taken Esme had obviously met up with three others. They were all headed the same way. The trail was wide and easy to follow as it looked like they hadn't been afraid of anyone following them so closely, or so soon. Even a blind man could have trailed them. Was that arrogance, or just pure laziness on their part, he wondered.

Cade knew that time was of the essence. What a group of ruffians would do to that pale little girl, he didn't want to think about. He just had to hope that they were going to hold out for a ransom. If that was the case, then they'd have to leave her unharmed.

Riding fast, Cade's eyes scanned the distance. He'd been told what to look out for. There. He could see the almost invisible rise in the land now. He'd been informed by Phillips, that the bluff was a dangerous place, almost unrecognizable until you rode over the edge. Then you'd never get home again. Going at the bluff from the opposite side, though, you might just about be able to see the narrow entrance. It was like a small, very deep, canyon. A deep slash in a huge and ancient rock, weathered and shaped over the millennia. A fissure, cut deep into the earth, aeons ago, and well disguised.

There was a scattering of sagebrush and rough scrub around the top, and a few boulders lined the edge. Not many hiding places for any rescuer. Once he was certain that that was the place, Cade stopped Sky and dismounted. He'd walk from here on in; the sound of a horse approaching too close could cause problems. Pulling the rope halter from the horse, Cade tucked it into his belt. He softly stroked the velvety nose of the big paint.

'OK Sky, you hang out hereabouts. I'll be back for you soon boy, don't worry.'

The horse, as if knowing he needed to be quiet, nuzzled his master's face gently. They'd been in similar situations, he wouldn't stray far. He snorted softly as Cade walked away from him, then bent to look for any sort of sparse grazing that may be around.

Cade headed for the bluff almost silently, crouching low, stopping behind the one or two large boulders that dotted the way, just in case there was a lookout. Though he doubted there would be; they'd feel they were safe in there and wouldn't have expected anyone to be following them up so soon.

He reached the top edge of the bluff and peered over. It was deep, and fairly narrow at the entrance, widening out to a rounded shape at the opposite end from the entrance, which was where the horses were kept. Anyone trying to get at the animals would have had to go right past the tumbledown shack which was built real close to the cliff face, and was a pretty rough affair, but with the shelter of the bluff around it, Cade reckoned it would be fairly strong and weatherproof.

His sharp eyes scanned around the area for a hiding place. A little way to his right, he could see there might be a way down to the shack. Precipitous, but, he knew he could make it — he'd done worse before. It was so steep in some places that he'd have to practically hang on by his fingertips. There were sharp outcrops, and vertical, flat planes of grey rock etched all about with lines and fissures.

There were some brave, small, stunted plants, clinging on to some of the outcrops and Cade marvelled at how they could find the wherewithal to grow up there. No one would ever have expected an intruder to come from that direction. At the top of the almost non-existent way down, there was a group of large, mixed boulders, rocks and scrub. An ideal hiding place. He shuffled quietly over to it, eased down into the cramped space and settled down to wait for whatever might come, and with it, a long, cold night.

From his vantage point, he could see the whole of the small skillet-shaped canyon. The horses were corralled at the wider end behind a rope fastened across from side to side, which was attached to stakes, crudely knocked into the rough ground. There were six animals.

He could hear the men inside the shack talking, although their words were indistinct, as they all seemed to be talking at once. He caught the odd words: 'Kill her', 'big ransom', 'do anything to get her back.' He feared for the girl, trapped in the shack with a gang of outlaws, who'd stop at nothing to get what they wanted. He couldn't begin to imagine Esme's fear and pain, but there was nothing at all that he could do yet. He needed to make sure he'd scouted out the place properly, and had a foolproof plan set up first.

He'd have to wait until dusk, couldn't risk getting any closer while it was still light enough for anyone to see him against the rocks. He could wait though, he'd been in tougher scrapes than this before now, and knew that it was almost always, simply a waiting game.

He froze, as one man left the shack and went over to the horses. Cade watched as he saddled one of them up. He thought he recognized the man, but from this position he really couldn't be sure. The outlaw led the animal to the entrance of the canyon and pulled aside the gate of sticks and brush that hid the entrance, then mounted and rode off.

Slowly, night began to creep over the edge of the bluff, the sky turning from brightest blue to denim, then navy, then, eventually, it was dark enough for Cade to attempt the dangerous climb down to the shack. He saw the light from lamps inside, and men were coming and going, laughing and talking, feeding and watering the horses. He could smell their food cooking. His belly was empty; it smelled darned good.

As soon as he knew that the five who were left were all inside the shack, Cade began slowly lowering himself down the steep side of the canyon, rooting for footholds and scrabbling for finger holds in the semi-darkness. A time or two he disturbed some loose scree and stones which went tumbling down into the canyon. When he did, he flattened against the stone wall and practically stopped breathing. But no one came out — they obviously hadn't heard the small noises he was making, over their talking and laughing.

Had someone come out and spotted him, he was in the most precarious position he'd ever been in. If the man who had ridden out from there earlier should happen to ride back in now, he'd most probably spot Cade, hanging on to the rocks like a monkey. Then Cade would be dead for sure. He couldn't reach for gun or knife without falling.

Someone had told him once that everyone had a guardian angel watching out for them. He sure hoped that his was with him tonight.

5

Cade eventually reached the floor of the canyon, quite close to the building, then flattened himself against the rock face and squeezed in tight behind the shack. It had taken him quite some time, and it was almost totally black down there now except for the slashes of yellow lamplight squeezing out from between the cracks and fissures in the walls of the cabin. He thanked his lucky stars that he wasn't any fatter, he'd never have fitted into the awkward gap between the jagged rocks, and the back of the rickety old building.

Moving slowly, so as to make as little noise as possible, he gradually eased his way round to where there was a chink of light squeezing itself out from between the timbers. Luckily it was at just about the right height for him to be able to peer into it without having to get himself into too uncomfortable a position.

Although the men inside were making enough noise not to have heard any small sound that Cade may have made, he was taking no chances. They felt safe way out here, he could see that. They felt there was no need for them to be quiet, or on guard, but it still wouldn't do to alert them to his presence in any way.

From his uncomfortable vantage point, Cade could see that three of them were playing cards on a rickety table. One looked to be asleep on a bunk to one side of the shack, and he could see what looked like the end of another bunk at the other side. He couldn't tell if the girl was there, though, it was just out of the range of his limited vision, given his cramped position, but it seemed probable she was.

A sudden noise, quite close by, made him hold his breath. One of the gang had left the shack, and come round it to the rock face to relieve himself. Thank goodness it was dark way back there, and night had closed in fast. Cade, in his dark clothing, blended in well with the rocks around him — he wouldn't be noticed.

The outlaw finished, sighed with relief, adjusted his clothing, and headed back into the bunkhouse. Cade breathed again, he'd counted five corralled horses from up on the bluff. He'd followed six loaded horses, one of which was Esme's. There were four men now in the shack with the girl; the other hadn't come back from wherever he'd ridden out to earlier in the evening.

Cade remained in his cramped and uncomfortable hideout at the rear of the building, listening and occasionally peering in through the gap. He was waiting for the opportune moment to make his move. The night drew in, and got colder. The men were cooking and eating, playing cards, laughing, talking loudly. He didn't hear a female voice yet. He hoped she was still alive.

Then he heard a horse riding in. Not in any hurry; the rider knew he wasn't being followed. The man casually unsaddled, tied his horse with the others and entered the shack. He wore a hat with a wide brim, and Cade, peering through the small crack couldn't see his face in the dim yellow lamplight. He felt certain, though, that he knew the man from somewhere, that he recognized the stand of him. He'd felt the same earlier, when he'd only been able to see the top of his head from his other vantage point, atop the high bluff. Cade fished about in his mind for a face to match the hat, but it wouldn't come to him, Suddenly his attention was drawn to the heated conversation which was now coming from the inside of the shack.

'You mean you ain't fed her yet? Or watered her? What in the hell you bin playin at!' Hushed, mumbled, guilty voices told both Cade and the obvious leader that, no, they hadn't either fed or watered the girl yet.

'Goddamn it! She ain't no good to us dead, you godforsaken sons of bitches! Get her up, give her a drink and some of that there bread. Move it! Or so help me you'll be out feedin' the buzzards in about twenty seconds!'

Cade had guessed right, those bunks he couldn't see from his hiding place were obviously where the girl was being held. One of the men went over and fished out a can of water from a barrel in the corner, then broke a chunk off the rough brown loaf on the table. He took them over to the bunks.

'Here, you, give me your hands, I'll loose 'em while you eat.'

Cade didn't hear the girl make any sort of sound, but his keen ears took in the harsh rasp of metal. Blast it! She was being kept chained up, not tied — that was a problem. Ropes he could cut in an instant; chains were another matter.

'So, what'd ole man Phillips say then, boss?' ventured one of the men.

The new arrival snorted derisively.

'Just told me, that if his girl was harmed in any way, 'people would suffer'!'

That remark was followed by raucous laughter.

'Yeah, if'n he can ever find us way out here, that is!'

'Sure, not even a pack rat could get in here without us knowin' about it, and if they did, they'd be goin' out dead!'

'Yeah. Well, one of you no-goods better get out there and do the rounds, just in case the stupid bastard's decided to try some sort of a rescue on his own!'

More loud, disbelieving, laughter followed that remark.

'Mickey, your turn.'

'Oh hell! I was just fixin' to get me some shut-eye now, boss!'

'It'll take you all of ten minutes, then you can shut your eyes just as long as you want. Go! Or I'll be shuttin' your eyes for you, permanent!'

There was a strong note of authority

to the voice — it was the sound of a man used to getting his own way, used to being obeyed. A chair scraped across the floor as the man rose to do his boss's bidding, huffing and puffing his indignant way to the door. Like a spoiled child, he slammed the old door hard behind him, shaking the whole structure of the tumble-down building and sending a shower of dust and debris all over Cade, and into his eyes. He could hear the man muttering curses under his breath, as he went to check that the horses were tied securely, before he sauntered across to check out the perimeter fence.

Cade wasn't worried that he'd be noticed. No one would ever think to look to the rear of a shack placed so close up against the rock face. Suddenly, he pricked up his ears as he heard the girl's voice, a quiet, heartbreaking sound in the dark of the night. There was a laugh from the men.

'Yeah, well, I guess so. Gotta keep you comfortable, eh? Waldo, take the little 'lady' outside, she needs to relieve herself.'

Cade could really feel the anger beginning to burn inside of him now. The way they were treating Esme was both embarrassing and barbaric. Maybe, though, this would be the chance he was looking for. But, as he listened, he could hear the movements of the girl and her captor: she was still chained. He couldn't possibly free her from the gang while she was chained, even if he could get close enough to grab her. That had put paid to his first plan. He heard the man and his captive coming round the side of the bunkhouse, right to the back end of the building. This was obviously their makeshift latrine.

'OK then, get on with it!'

Waldo's voice was rough and hard. Esme was standing right beside the back corner of the building, only feet away from Cade. He could have reached right out and touched her. He silenced his breathing, and froze. He could see her, but would she also see him and, believing him to be one of the gang, cry out in fear? He could see the heavy chains around her ankles and her wrists, which were attached to a longer one that the outlaw was holding the end of. Cade kept as still as the rocks he was pressed against.

She spoke in a weak, shaky voice.

'Please, can you turn your back? I can't . . . not with you . . . please?'

She stood quietly, head bowed. Waldo sneered.

'Wassa matter, bitch? Can't perform in public? Look, woman, I've seen all you've got to offer, and more besides, so don't you worry yourself about embarrassing me,' he chuckled roughly.

Cade's anger swelled. He wanted to just go out there and break the man's neck, but he knew it wouldn't do any of them any good. He needed to be able to unfasten her chains; they couldn't go anywhere with her still chained up like that. He forced himself to be calm.

'Please, Mr Waldo, for the sake of

common decency, do please turn your back.'

'Decency, that's a pretty, high falutin' word, Missy ain't it? But I guess I better do as I'm asked, else we'll be here all bloody night, now go on.'

He must have turned his back at last, as Cade saw the girl lift her skirts. He turned his head away and waited until he heard the quiet rustle of her petticoats that told him she was adjusting her clothes. Then, turning back towards her, he gave a small hiss, and quickly reached his finger to his lips. She jumped as if she'd been bitten, and looked around her fearfully. She spotted Cade in the shadows. Quickly, he shook his head.

Somehow, perhaps due to the streak of light coming through the cracks in the wood of the shed, she must have recognized him, and she calmed down. He reached as far out towards her as was possible, given the constriction of the rocks and cabin, and whispered to her as low as he could.

'I'll get you out of here, Miss Esme, don't you worry. Just you try and hold on a little while longer. I'm right here.'

She smiled weakly at him, but her eyes lit up: here was her saviour. She'd endure the outlaws' taunts a while longer without a sound now she knew she was to be rescued. A pull on the chain around her ankle jerked her off her feet, and she fell to her knees with a grunt.

'What's that? You finished? Come on then, get up, or I'll just drag you back to your bed through the dirt. Come on, woman.'

He pulled her forcibly to her feet, and dragged and pushed her back indoors, the rasping of the chain telling Cade that she was once again chained fast to the bunk.

'My pa, he'll send people out to save me, you know. He'll never pay any of you. You'll not get one red cent.'

Her voice was shaking, but Cade had to admit, she had some guts, facing up to them all in her situation.

'No? Well we'll just see 'bout that. And hey, sweetheart, no pay, no darlin' daughter back. But hey, we'll all be havin' some pretty fun with a tasty little filly like you before we slit your throat, won't we boys? Gag her, Waldo. Can't be doin' with bloody jabberin' women.'

'Oh, boss, can't we play with her now?' one of the outlaws asked, in a childlike voice.

Loud, raucous laughter followed that remark. Cade, in his hiding place, and completely helpless to do anything for her yet, seethed, shaking with pent-up anger.

'Snake! What'd I just say? We leave her be unless the old man doesn't pay up, then she's fair game. He pays up, we send her home, unharmed, we're off to Mexico, rich, free men, all the women we want. Daddy doesn't pay, and he gets back a bloody, used up corpse!'

Cade's blood was boiling. His thought, right then, was simply to go in shooting, with both irons, but that'd probably get the girl killed anyway. He had to do some hard thinking; he needed to straighten this out, but the anger wouldn't let him. Esme was still alive and unharmed, up to now, and the gang wouldn't hurt her unless they didn't get the money.

There were still a few more hours until sunup, which was when, he reckoned, one of them would be riding out to collect the money.

Cade forced himself to be calm then. Gradually, he silenced the devil that was seething within, climbed carefully back up to his hiding place above the shack, and started to plan.

6

Come sunup, the first man to wake stoked up the old black stove, placed the pot of coffee on top and went outside to relieve himself. A loud shout soon had the others leaping up, and reaching for their guns, staggering, sleepy-eyed and blinking like owls out into the already bright day. They all ran about like ants.

'The goddamn horses've gone! They've all gone, every last one of 'em!'

'How in the hell?'

'Who the — Who did that? How?'

'Boss, you rode back late last night, you must've left the rope loose.'

'What you sayin'? You blamin' me for this, Snake?'

'I'm just sayin' as you were last man in is all, they were all there when I checked 'em before you got back here!'

A single shot rang round the small

canyon. Snake fell to his knees, then slowly collapsed on to his face, a single bullet between the eyes. The gun was still smoking; blood splattered against the wall of the cabin.

'Anyone else blamin' me?' There was, of course, no response. 'Good, if there's any goddamn blame at all, it's on Mikey, ain't it. I told him to check 'em after I got in. Is there any reason to doubt he didn't do his job right?' The men were silent. 'Good. Now, the lot of you, get out there and find them there animals, Mikey, you take care of Snake, I'll wait right here with the girl. Move it!'

He fired another round into the air. It galvanized them all into action, and they began to run about looking for the lost animals. Mikey dragged Snake over to the side of the shack and unceremoniously dumped him there, then ran off to help the other three to look for the horses.

The narrow entrance to the small canyon was blocked with a thick brushwood fence and gate. The gate was gaping open. The horses were usually fastened to a thick rope across the further, wider, end of the canyon, beyond the bunkhouse. That rope was lying on the ground now. The leader wandered over to look at it. Cut. Not untied. He knew he'd left it right last night, and Mikey, the youngest of the gang, had checked it after he'd got in, reporting all was well.

Who could have sneaked in and cut the rope without being heard, and without the horses making a sound? Injuns? Nope, they'd have come in after the scalps too. Mebbe old man Phillips had sent someone after the girl after all? But how in the hell could they have gotten in, and out again, with six horses, without being heard? He took off his broad-brimmed hat and scratched his head, looking around the canyon, and upwards.

The man hiding up in the patch of brush at the top of the bluff took a breath and stiffened as he recognized the leader of the kidnappers at last. Of course! He'd known that hat, the stance, even the voice, but until this moment he hadn't been able to place them all together on one man. It was Sheriff Gerrard himself.

'Shit!' This would take even more careful handling than he'd planned for. He couldn't kill the sheriff. He needed to re-think, quick. Meantime, he could even the odds up, just a little, by dispatching one or two of the other guys. Gerrard had nicely helped by getting rid of one of them for a start, which just left three others, and Gerrard himself, for him to take care of now.

Cade crept carefully down the rocks, at the end of the canyon, taking care not to dislodge any scree or stones as he went. He sheltered behind boulders and shrubs, waiting round the rocks for one of the men to come close enough to him. That unfortunate man lived for all of a minute after Cade had slashed the guy's throat in one swift, deep, strike.

The man grabbed at his throat with both of his hands, trying to shout, blood gushing from the single, fatal wound as he dropped to his knees, then on to his face in the dust.

Cade quickly pulled the dead man round a boulder, so that he wouldn't be immediately seen, kicked dust and grit over the bloodstain to disguise it and went back to his hiding place on an overhanging section of rock. Two more men were left now. Gerrard had to be kept alive to answer for his deeds back in town. Crouching as low as he could, bloodied knife still clutched in his hand, Cade waited for the next man to appear.

When the second outlaw came around the rocks looking for the horses, not knowing his companion was dead, he lived just a little longer, trying to shout for help, but unable to, as his life blood drained from the deep wound across his jugular. Cade piled that body unceremoniously atop the other, and went to wait for his next victim.

The anger was in full flow now, yet some common sense was still lurking deep in there somewhere; he needed Gerrard alive, as well as little Esme. He knew there had been four men, as well as the sheriff. One had been killed by his boss; Cade had killed two now, so there was just one more to account for, and then he'd have to face down the sheriff.

He heard the buzzards starting to keen high above; the scent of so much blood carried far on the still morning air. He just had to hope that the outlaws' ears were not as well tuned into the sound as his were. If they'd heard it too, he'd have to be extra careful, but some way or other, he had to capture Gerrard alive, and get him, and Miss Esme, back to Kicking Horse.

How he was going to do it, he didn't know right at that moment. As soon as the sheriff knew he was being stalked, he'd be on the lookout, and a hunted man is a dangerous man. Cade's anger had him so fired up, he hadn't been able to reason straight. He needed to calm himself down, now, and think some. He climbed back up to his hiding place again. They wouldn't look up there — they'd believe that only an Injun could climb that steep outcrop. The outlaws could never have climbed it. None was as fit or honed as Cade, and none was as fired up, or flying high as the eagle, angry as hell. Hot, red anger, fearless anger, surging through his veins, driving him onward.

Just then, he heard horses. The last remaining man had found some of the runaways, and was leading them back. Cade watched as the man tied the animals up behind the shack at end of the canyon, and then headed back for the shack. He was just too far away for Cade to throw his knife with any real accuracy, so he held back, and the man entered the shack.

There was just the one man with the sheriff in there now. Cade was more than happy with those odds. But he knew that Esme was still chained to the bed. Then he heard angry voices, things being thrown about, crashing and splintering. He could hear the sheriff stomping around, cussing about the fools he'd hired, and how he should just kill the girl and have done with it. The shouting increased in volume, the man, Waldo, insisting that they should just use the girl, then kill her, and ride away.

'And how in hell do you suggest we do that, you stupid son of a whore! There's a crazy sonofabitch out there killin' off any of us that show our faces.' He paused. 'Crazy! Damn it! I know who it is! It's that Cade guy, 'Crazy Man Cade' they call him. He was in town this week. He was at the Phillips house for tea the same night I was there, we were introduced. Holy shit, if it's him, we've really got one hell of a problem.'

Waldo taunted the sheriff then.

'What's that, Gerrard? You scared of some guy just coz he's got a stupid name? He's only one man, on his own. We can take him out.'

'Are you not listening to me, you stupid sonofabitch? I've heard about this guy, he's a mad crazy killer, stops at nothin' to get whoever he's after, shows no mercy, and never fails. We're in bloody big trouble I tell you!'

It sounded to Cade as if Gerrard had lost his nerve — that was good news. As Waldo carried on taunting Gerrard, a single shot rang out, followed by total silence. Then someone began moving things around, and throwing furniture aside. Cade heard the sheriff talking to the girl, though he couldn't quite catch what he was saying to her. So now, there was just the sheriff left — that was even better.

Cade could imagine Esme, chained and gagged, watching the sheriff pacing about and listening to his words. Cade knew how afraid she must be, seeing Waldo killed in front of her, probably believing she was going to be shot, or worse, right about now. The sheriff couldn't very well take her back to town and say he'd rescued her; she'd heard and seen everything, and now he knew there was someone out there who really was here to rescue her.

They'd just have to fight it out. Sheriff Gerrard reckoned he was pretty quick with an iron, but his opponent had the advantage of being hidden somewhere up there in the rocks. He'd have to call him out, but Gerrard considered that he had the upper hand; his opponent wouldn't fire on him, in case he hit the girl. The sheriff would use her as a living shield, ride away with her, and when they were far enough away, either kill her, or just leave her wandering around some place for the buzzards to find.

'We'll see if you get back home alive, missy.'

The chains rasped against the bed frame, as the sheriff released the girl. A few moments later Gerrard came out of the shack. He was holding the girl in front of him with one hand, and his gun in the other, looking around the canyon. Esme's hands were chained behind her back, and she had a gag stuffed in her mouth. Her blue dress was dirty and torn, her blonde curls hung in an untidy, dirty mess and she had bruises, dirt and scratches on her pale cheeks. Her wide eyes were filled with tears. Cade seethed, but stayed still. Gerrard shouted out loud, his voice echoing around the canyon.

'Come on out and face me, you coward! Face me like a real man, Cade. It is you, isn't it, Cade? I'm calling you out right now. C'mon, let's see just how 'Crazy' you really are, huh? But then I guess you really must be damned crazy, coming in here single-handed to try and rescue the little lady?'

Esme shook her head frantically, the sheriff let go of her, and hit her round the head, almost knocking her off her feet.

'You just be still there, missy. I'm gonna kill this nuisance. I'll have my way with you, then kill you, and take you and this Cade feller back to town and tell 'em all it was this crazy bastard that did it. How'd you like that idea, Cade, huh?'

He looked around. There was no sound. He fired into the air, the noise ricocheting around the small canyon, and making the horses shy in fear.

'Get out here, you bloody coward! Out where I can see you!'

Still Cade held his silence. That seemed to annoy the older man even more, and Cade really liked to annoy people. Gerrard fired off another round aimlessly. Cade was counting. Gerrard put his gun to Esme's head. Cade could see the tears streaking the dirt on her face. Her eyes were wide and terrified and she couldn't make much sound because of the gag, but Cade could tell she'd be screaming if she could.

'OK come on out, mister, or the girl dies, here, now.'

He pulled back the hammer on his Colt, the clicks sounding like shots in the hollow air of the small canyon.

'You've got to the count of five,

mister, then she goes back to Daddy in pieces. One.'

Gerrard pushed Esme forward hard, and she fell on her face in the dirt. He drew a second gun from its holster. He placed one foot hard into the middle of Esme's back, holding her down, as he looked around him.

'You know you can't kill me, Cade. That's two. How would it look, killing a sheriff in pursuit of his duty? You wouldn't be a very popular man anywhere then, would you. Three.'

He fired up into the bushes where Cade was hiding, almost hitting him, still Cade stayed his hand.

'That's four. The little lady ain't got much time left now, Cade. Where are you, you bastard? Show yourself!'

Gerrard looked around the canyon seeking out likely hiding places. The sun was close on its zenith, and as he looked upward, he was almost blinded by the beam of sudden harsh white light appearing over the rocks. A single shot rang out, and the full gun flew from his hand. Instinctively he grabbed at the smashed and bleeding hand with the other, not dropping that gun, but pulling the bleeding hand close into his chest. He stepped forward, leaving Esme lying on the ground, and heading towards his other gun.

Cade's next bullet hit Gerrard in the leg. As he fell, he fired upward. By a stroke of complete luck, his bullet grazed Cade's shoulder. Gerrard was crawling forward to try and reach his other gun, knowing he was almost out of slugs in his first one. Cade fired again, the bullet throwing up a cloud of dust into the sheriff's eyes.

Esme was still lying in the dirt, eyes wildly searching for her saviour, as the sheriff spat and swore, and tried to clear the sand from his eyes. By the time he could finally see, Cade had jumped down from his hiding place, and stood in front of him, one foot on top of Gerrard's lost gun, and with both of his own guns drawn and cocked, both aimed squarely at the sheriff.

'OK, now, Sheriff, you drop that gun, and sit there quietly, while I go and untie Miss Esme. You know I don't want to kill you.'

'No, but I damn well want to kill you, Cade!'

Gerrard raised himself up, and fired up at Cade, who blasted a hole in the other man's shoulder with practised ease. Gerrard fell back to the floor, grabbing at his shoulder with his good hand. Cade towered over him.

'Give me the key to her chains, Gerrard. NOW!'

Gerrard used his good hand to fumble in his pocket, and produced the key, which he flicked up at Cade, who, with lightning fast reflexes, slicked one gun back into its cradle and caught the key mid spin. He picked up both of the sheriff's guns and shoved them into his belt, leaving Gerrard squirming in the dirt, whilst he went over and unchained Esme, pulling the dirty gag from her mouth. She sat up and grabbed hold of him tightly, pulling him to her and sobbing.

'Thank you, Mr Cade, oh thank you so much. I was terrified of what they might do to me. Did you really come alone?'

She looked frantically around the canyon.

'Sure did. Anyone else would just have slowed me down, miss, and I guessed I needed to get out here real quick.'

Esme's eye's widened as she looked behind Cade. He turned instantly, pushing Esme away from him unceremoniously. Gerrard was on his feet, dragging his wounded leg, and was close behind Cade, hands outstretched to grab him. Cade kicked out in the same instant that he turned, and the toe of his boot landed right between Gerrard's legs, doubling him up, so that he fell forward into the dust.

Cade picked Esme up from where she'd landed, unfastened the chains from her wrists and ankles and took them over to Gerrard, fastening his hands behind him tightly, and ignoring the man's protests of the pain in his shot hand, arm and leg.

'You'll live, Gerrard, don't worry — long enough to face a jury, anyways. Shame though, I really would've liked to put an end to you myself. Very, very, slowly.'

He roughly jerked the man to his feet, and pushed him in front of him over to the cabin. Esme followed closely. He chained Gerrard to the bed, and gagged him. He pushed the body of the dead outlaw who the sheriff had shot earlier, over into a corner, out of the eyeline of the girl.

'OK now, Miss Esme, can you use a gun?'

'Sure, Poppa taught me how to shoot when I was just a kid.' She noticed the blood slowly spreading over Cade's shoulder. 'You're hurt! Let me see to it.'

Cade thrust one of the sheriff's pistols into her small hand. She looked up at him, frowning.

'Thank you, Miss Esme, but it's just a flesh wound. I'll be fine until we get into town. Now, if'n he makes a wrong move, you just shoot him, I don't much care where you shoot him, just try your best not to kill him is all; he's got to go back to answer for what he's done. Are you feelin' well enough to ride?'

She nodded, dusty blonde hair tangling around her shoulders even more.

'Sure. Why?'

'I'm goin' out to saddle up some horses to get us home, I won't be long, you OK to watch him till I get back with the horses? Then we'll get on back to town and your poppa.'

'Oh yes please. I'll be fine, Mr Cade.' Her voice quivered, 'Please, don't be long, though.'

She sat on a chair facing Gerrard, pointing the gun at him, shaking a little, but with a hard stare in her eyes, which left Cade, and probably Gerrard, in no doubt at all, that she would sure as hell use that gun if she needed to.

Cade found the tackle, bridled and saddled up the three best looking animals, putting rope halters on the other two and fastening them to the pommels of two of the saddled horses. When he returned to the cabin, the two people he'd left there were still in the same places, the big Colt looked like a cannon in Esme's small hand, but her grip was steadier now. Sheriff Gerrard was frowning, and gazing at his boots intently. Cade smiled.

'Well this sure is a sight. I sure wish your pa could see you now, Miss Esme.'

She smiled disarmingly up at him.

'I've really got you to thank that my Poppa will see me again at all, Mr Cade.'

Cade crossed the cabin, and unfastened the chains, pulling the sheriff unceremoniously to his feet, and making certain that the chains were tight enough behind his back. Esme quickly made to give him the gun back.

'No, miss, until we're back in Kicking Horse, you just hold on to it. You don't know what might happen out there, this guy's a sidewinder and he could try anything. The more guns on him the better. My own horse is waiting out there somewhere — I'll change horses when we reach him. I'll need you to watch Gerrard for us then.'

He pushed Gerrard out of the cabin and over to the horses, helped Esme up onto the smaller of them, pushed the groaning sheriff up onto one of the others, and grabbed its reins. Smoothly then, he mounted one of the other horses, and kicked the animal on, pulling on the reins of the sheriff's horse. With Esme following closely, they headed out of the canyon, back towards Kicking Horse.

Around a mile or so out of the canyon, a small group of apparently wild horses were to be seen. Cade stood tall in his stirrups and shaded his eyes to take a closer look at the group, then let out a resounding whistle. Esme watched as one of the group broke off, and headed at a trot towards them, head up, ears forward. As it approached them, she could see that it was a big paint. It headed straight for Cade and stopped in front of the animal he was riding.

'Miss Esme, you OK to watch Gerrard, while I sort my horse out?'

'I sure am,' she smiled, and levelled the gun at the sheriff's head.

The horses greeted one another, muzzle to muzzle with long slow sniffs, as Cade dismounted from the chestnut he'd been riding and greeted his own horse, pulling the rope halter from his belt, and placing it over Sky's head. The paint stood quite still.

'Don't worry, Sky old feller, we'll soon get back to town. This'll have to do for now.' Cade grabbed the reins of the chestnut, swung easily up on to the wide bare back of his coloured mount and led the small group onward.

'Mr Cade, can I ask you something please?'

Esme was riding as close to him as was possible now.

'Miss?'

'You didn't — well — you didn't ride out here bareback just to come and get me, did you?'

'Sure did, quicker this way, then I can just let my horse loose to fend for himself until I need him, or, if'n by some chance, I don't come back to him, well, he'll be OK in the wild with no tack to slow him down.'

Esme's eyes widened, her opinion of this man had changed radically: he was brave and he was fearless and she knew now that she could trust him with her life. She blessed the day that he'd come into her life. Maybe, just maybe, he'd like to get to know her better after all this was over. She sure hoped so.

The sheriff groaned. Esme pointed her gun at him.

'You got something to say, mister?'

Her voice was hard as flint. Cade smiled; she had some guts for such a little girl.

Sheriff Gerrard shook his bowed head and was silent again. Cade stifled a smile. She was an ornery little madam, sassy, but pretty with it, he would like to bet she'd turn many a head. But, despite her guts in a sticky situation, he had realized that she really wasn't his type, so as soon as he'd seen her settled back with her pa, got his own shoulder fixed and gotten the sheriff jailed, he'd be leaving Kicking Horse. Fast.

He was getting just a little tired of finding himself in these sticky situations.

*　*　*

Cade, Esme and the sheriff rode out to the Phillips ranch first, where George Phillips saw them riding in and rushed out to meet them. Esme leaped from her horse almost before it had stopped, and rushed to her father. They held on to one another so tightly Cade wondered if they weren't going to break one another's bones.

Cade held on to Gerrard's horse as

they watched the reunion. Esme told her father all about what had gone on, and when he turned back to face the two men, his face was dark and twisted with anger. He stepped away from his daughter, and pointed his finger up at the cowed figure of the former sheriff.

'You, Gerrard! You're a bloody disgrace to the badge! Mr Cade here and I are going to stick you in the caboose, and then I'm going to be telegraphing over to Jemson to get their sheriff to come on over and do the necessary. It's only thanks to Mr Cade that I don't just damn well kill you right now!'

Cade nodded in agreement.

'I was sore tempted to do just that, George, believe me. When I saw what state Miss Esme was in, I could've wrung his scrawny bloody neck and pulled him apart with my bare hands, but I reckoned it was best that he stands in front of the law that he's supposed to represent. Don't know if'n he'll hang for what he's done, but he'll sure as hell go away for a long time.'

Phillips called out for Conchita to come and take care of Esme. They greeted one another with hugs and tears and Conchita wrapped a shawl around the girl's shoulders and took her quickly into the house. Phillips watched as they went indoors, then went across to the stable and saddled up his horse. He led Gerrard and Cade out from the ranch towards town. Around halfway to town, Phillips halted and turned in the saddle. He was pointing his gun at Gerrard, his eyes cold and deadly. Cade pushed his horse forward to stand between them.

'No, George, you know he ain't worth it. You know that. Come on. Miss Esme's goin' to be fine, honest. He didn't hurt her any.'

'Didn't hurt her! Did you see the state of her? Did you see the look in her eyes, Jed, did you? My daughter was terrified; she looked like a little trapped bird. I can't stand to see her look like that. And it's all *his* doing! Hell is too good for this goddamn sonofabitch, I can tell you.' He cocked his gun and pointed it directly, point blank at Cade.

'I'll go through you if I have to, Cade, believe me. I don't want to, I think a hell of a lot of you for what you've done for my family, but I swear I *will* go through you. Now you move aside, and let me at him.'

Cade simply shook his head again.

'Can't do that, George. You're a better man than that, we both know it. If'n you kill him, then you're worse than him. I know for certain that apart from frightening her, and makin' her a bit uncomfortable, him and his gang never did nothing to Miss Esme for her to be ashamed about. I was there most of the time, hidin' real close, and watchin' them. Sure, she was chained up, but what good would it have done them to harm her? She's gonna be fine. Let's just get Gerrard in to town and forget this happened, eh? Put your gun away, George. Please, for your daughter's sake. She wouldn't want to see you hung for murderin' a lawman would she?'

Phillips shamefacedly replaced his gun in its holster, and started to ride ahead. Gerrard turned to Cade.

'Thanks for that.'

'Shut the hell up, Gerrard, and ride, or *I'm* gonna be the one to put a bullet in your back. I'm not Phillips, so I ain't got no reason on earth not to. Now move it.'

The sorry trio reached the town, and escorted Gerrard to the jailhouse. The deputy, Luke Chaney, was hanging about and, with a look of total bewilderment on his face, handed the jail key to Phillips, recognizing the authority in the man's voice as Phillips and Cade locked Gerrard in the jail cell, and went back into the office. Phillips took Cade to one side.

'I'm a tad concerned about leaving Chaney in charge here. He's a no-good drunkard, might easily let the bastard out before the law can get over here from Jemson, and I — well — I want to get back as quick as possible to my Esme.'

He looked long and hard at Cade. Cade knew exactly what he was asking. Oh, what the hell, he was in no hurry to go anywhere.

'OK George, for you and your daughter, I'll hang on in here 'till the Jemson sheriff arrives, then I'm off.'

Phillips clapped him on the back. 'Good man, I'm in your debt, yet again. It should only be for a couple of days, then you can get off on your travels again. Though I reckon Esme won't be too happy 'bout that. You go see the doc first, though, and get that shoulder looked at. Don't want it getting infected huh?'

Phillips smiled and pushed his hat down on his head. He left the jailhouse, crossed over to the telegraph office to send his message, then returned and mounted up, riding as fast as he could to get back home to his girl.

Three days later, Cade was relieved by the sheriff from Jemson, and after giving his version of the tale, he explained to the sheriff that George Phillips would be able to give him another version of the tale, along with his daughter's. Now that the sheriff was here, Cade offered to ride on over to their ranch and get George and his daughter out to the town as soon as they could get there.

Cade was mighty relieved to be finished with his duties. Even though there had been no trouble while he'd been in the town, he was uncomfortable in the role of temporary sheriff, couldn't wait to get out of town, and up into the cold of the mountains once more. He rode Sky at speed out to the Phillips ranch. Esme ran out to meet him.

'Mr Cade! Hello again. Thank you so very much for what you did for me — it's truly wonderful to see you again. Is your shoulder better? Won't you come in? Please?'

Cade sensed trouble. This girl was a pretty one, but he realized that he had no real feeling for her, in fact, she didn't make him feel anything at all. He knew he had to get away from here as soon as possible, before she began to think otherwise. He shook his head as he looked down at her eager features.

'Shoulder's just fine, thanks, but no, Miss Esme, I won't be comin' in. Glad to see you're OK again. I reckon my job's done now; it's high time I was headed off on my travels again.'

The look of pain in her eyes almost made his heart melt, but he hardened his resolve.

'I'll escort you and your pa into town now to see the sheriff from Jemson, so you can give him the facts as you know them, then I'm gonna be off. Too many folks around here, makes me tight, uncomfortable, I need to be alone. That's just my way. Sorry, Miss Esme, but, well — I just wouldn't fit in here. Go, fetch your pa, saddle up, and we'll get off.'

Esme burst into tears, turned on her

heels and ran back to the house. Some minutes later, she returned with her father, her tears dried, they were both dressed for riding. They went to the stables and tacked up their mounts, then joined Cade in the front yard. They all rode out, in silence, towards the town. When they arrived at the jailhouse, they tied their mounts to the hitching rail.

Cade entered the office first, in time to see the sheriff from Jemson with his gun pointing at the cowering prisoner, and deputy Chaney lying, apparently unconscious on the floor. Quickly, Cade pushed Esme and her father back out of the jailhouse.

'Stay out there, both of you, and don't come in until I come for you. Stay!'

He went in and closed the door quickly behind himself.

'Sheriff! What in the hell are you doin'? That man's got to stand trial. You can't do that, not to an unarmed man.'

The sheriff turned, the gun pointed

at Cade, who resisted drawing his own in turn.

'Good job you came in when you did, Mr Cade, or this snake'd have been meetin' his Maker by now.'

'So I see, but why?'

'Him and this no-good sonofabitch so-called deputy,' he kicked Chaney where he lay on the floor, 'they were windin' me up. It kinda got to me, so I slugged Chaney. But hey, how's about I just put Chaney in with him, lock the door on them both and forget them until the Justice arrives, he's due here in a day or two, if'n they've killed one another when the Justice gets here, saves him a job, huh?'

He shrugged, shamefacedly looking at the floor, and slowly lowered his gun. Cade smiled at the man; he knew he was a good man, he'd just been pushed by the constant jibing from Gerrard, whom, Cade knew, had the gift of talking people to anger.

'That's better, sir. Let's go out front, away from his jibes.'

He steered the sheriff out into the front office, gently putting his hand on the man's gun hand, and directing his iron back into its holster. Cade went and fetched Phillips and his daughter in. They all sat at the desk and the sheriff took notes as they all discussed the case.

'Right, well I sure think there's enough here for the Justice now, thank you all.'

The sheriff stood, and Phillips and his daughter both followed suit and headed for the door, Esme turning to look back at Cade. Her eyes were filled with longing, and tears. He got his comment in before she could say a word.

'I'll be heading off on my business now, folks. Maybe I'll call in again when I'm passin' here next time.'

He saw the look on Esme's face. Her father took hold of her elbow, and escorted her away from the office.

'We owe you our thanks, Mr Cade — Jed — many times over. Know that you will always be welcome at our home, whenever you should happen to be 'passing'. And I meant what I said. If I can ever be of any help to you, in any way at all, you know where I live.'

He tipped his hat and escorted his daughter to their mounts, then helped her up, and they rode off. Cade went back into the office, and sat back at the desk with the sheriff.

'OK, Sheriff, I'm headin' off any time. I am right in thinkin' that Gerrard and his crony will be safe here until the Justice arrives, ain't I?'

He raised his eyebrows at the man, who glanced down at his desk and spoke quietly.

'I know, it was a moment of weakness, and it won't be happening again. Don't worry, Mr Cade and thanks for your help. If'n you'd like me to deputize you properly, you could stick around a while longer and help me out.'

Cade shook his head emphatically.

'Nope, don't reckon so, thanks. I'm

missin' the mountains, need to get back up there. You'll be fine, there's some real good men living in this here town. You and the Justice will be able to employ a new sheriff, and a deputy, who won't take advantage of the town folks like Gerrard did. I'll be going now, sir.'

Touching his hat in salute to the man, Cade left the office. Mounting Sky quickly, he headed out of the town fast, up towards the mountains where he could breathe the good fresh air again.

8

Cade sucked the fresh, cold air of the mountains deep into his lungs and sighed. This was where he belonged, not down in the towns; he really needed the silence for his anger to stay in control. He was at peace up here. The only people who could get at him were his old friend, Bear, and the Indians. That suited him well.

He kept on riding until he was a long day or so away from the town of Kicking Horse, and began scouting around for a place he could stop for the night. He soon had himself and Sky settled in and a fire up and burning well enough for a billy of coffee. He began to prepare a small meal for himself.

All of a sudden, Cade froze — he knew he was being watched. But this time he didn't believe it was Bear. There was a subtle difference. He could tell the difference somehow. He carried on cooking his meal, going about things as if all was fine, while all the time listening, tuning in his ears to pick up all of the sounds and mentally listing them as he recognized them.

There, that was a deer, high-stepping through the undergrowth, birds singing, the small stream bubbling and flowing over the stones close by. He could even hear a rustling in the carpet of fallen leaves, and recognized it as a snake, sinuously, steadfastly, following its prey. But he didn't hear again whatever it had been that had startled him.

It was warm so close to the cooking fire, and Cade rolled up his sleeves, exposing his strong forearms. The long, thick white scar stood out against his weather-browned skin, as it twisted its tortuous way from his elbow and around his forearm to the wrist. He wore a thick leather wristband, but that couldn't hide the scar. He didn't notice it himself now, he'd lived with it for so long. But it gleamed, bone-white against his flesh, and was obvious to anyone once his sleeves were rolled up, or his shirt discarded. Many a woman had commented on it whilst lying in his strong arms. He always passed it off, saying it was simply the result of a fight. No need to tell them all the details.

As he settled down to eat his sparse meal, he again became aware of the feeling of being watched, but not by any animal — they were human eyes that were fixed on him. Despite continuing to eat his food, his muscles were tightly-coiled, ready to move at a moment's notice. Those eyes were on him all through his meal. It definitely wasn't Bear; he'd have been out for the food by now, he could never resist the smell of someone else's food being cooked.

Cade took his utensils down to the river, and washed them, taking his time, strolling back and placing them beside the fire to dry. He settled down beside the fire, knowing the person in the trees was still out there. He decided the time was right now to challenge them. If they'd meant him any harm, they'd had plenty of chances, but they hadn't made a move, so there was no threat.

Still sitting calmly beside the fire, he picked up a stick, and started to stir the ash about, stirring up gold and white sparks which scattered and flew up into the darkening sky. Still making no attempt to look around, he spoke.

'Why don't you come over and share the fire, mister? It's gettin' cold out there.'

A rustling noise behind him made Cade reach for his gun, surreptitiously. A low sound came from behind the wide bole of an old tree. A shadow appeared, turning itself into . . . an Indian brave! Cade's gun was out faster than a blink. The Indian stopped, and stood dead still between the tree and Cade, holding his hands down by his sides, palms out and open, to show he carried no weapons.

Cade could see by the breech-clout and leggings, and the long braids he wore, that this was an Arapaho. Most probably friendly, but it didn't do to take any chances. His quick eyes took in the fact that the newcomer was carrying a tomahawk and a large knife, but both were in place, firmly in his belt. Cade nodded at his visitor, replaced the Colt loosely into the holster and held his hands out in imitation of the other.

He was puzzled. This Indian had come looking for him, but why? He did speak some words for some of the tribes, but couldn't remember much Arapaho, right when he needed it most. He pointed to himself, 'Cade.' The Indian nodded and smiled. Now then, was that the smile of a man who'd just found a friend, or one of a man who knew this was the right man to kill?

The warrior pointed to himself, 'Bee-xoo-kuu.' Cade recognized that word, it made him smile. Surely an Arapaho warrior hadn't been named 'Pack Rat'. The Indian frowned, Cade straightened his face, he still didn't know what the red man wanted. He motioned towards the fire. '*Cee-noku*, sit,' he said hesitantly, not sure if the word was right.

The man smiled, and walked slowly, silently, over towards Cade, sitting himself down on a log, and warming his hands at the fire. Cade knew it was polite to wait until the man was ready, and let him speak in his own time, unless he was to have the Indian think he was in danger.

The man looked carefully at Cade, running his dark eyes over every inch of the big white man before him. His eyes fixed on the scar on his arm, and Cade absently found himself fingering it. He picked up a dry branch to place on the fire, and as he leaned forward, the large bear tooth on his neck thong showed over the collar of his shirt. The Indian smiled broadly, and nodded, pointing to the tooth. Cade grabbed at it, thinking the Indian wanted it.

'Wo-xuu, Wo-xuu!' the Indian cried. 'Cade — Wo-xuu *ciini'ouubeiht*!'

Cade knew the word Wo-xuu meant

'Bear'. Did his visitor want the huge bear tooth, or was there something wrong with Bear?

'Wo-xuu?' He shrugged, and frowned, not really understanding. The brave cast his eyes around, thinking how he could say what was needed. Then, without preliminaries, he threw himself to the ground, grabbed his stomach and writhed about groaning, acting as if he was vomiting. Cade really didn't know what was going on. Was the man dying? If he was, what could Cade do with the body? How did you bury an Arapaho? Should he just leave him here for his tribe to find? 'Wo-xuu,' groaned the Indian. Then he stood up and faced Cade, apparently none the worse for wear. He pointed to Cade, to the bear tooth, then to himself, then into the trees.

'Cade — *Bee-xoo-kuu, sooxoe* Wo-xuu!' There was an urgency in his voice.

All at once Cade saw the light. He grabbed the Indian by the shoulder, took the bear tooth in one hand, and waved it at him.

'Have I got you right, mister? Bear — Wo-xuu — he's sick, right? You want me to go with you to help him? Wo-xuu — sick?'

He clutched his stomach. The Indian nodded emphatically, smiling fit to bust, pleased that he'd at last got his message across. Cade quickly packed up his camp, loaded his horse, and motioned to the warrior.

'OK Pack Rat, lead the way.'

The Indian frowned. Cade pointed in the direction from which the Indian had come.

'Wo-xuu — GO!'

At once Bee-xoo-kuu turned quickly into the trees, and began to lead the way. For those who knew what to look for, the path was clear to see. Cade was leading Sky; he couldn't have ridden in these woods. Some way into the trees, they reached a small clearing where there was a rangy-looking Indian pony tied to one of the trees. Pack Rat untied him and carried on along the path, leading his own horse.

166

When they reached the edge of the treeline, they stopped. Cade turned to the man beside him, he'd thought Bear was near.

'*Bee-xoo-kuu too-tii-siihi?* Where is it?'

The Indian pointed out toward the horizon. Cade narrowed his eyes; there was a thin dark line of green, it must be trees for them to be able to see the green from here, and from them, a thin snake of grey smoke was rising into the open sky.

The Indian shrugged, 'Wo-xuu,' nodded and pointed to the smoke. Cade mounted Sky, and with the Indian on his pony close behind, urged him into a fast gallop. If Bear was ill, he needed to get there fast. He didn't believe it was a trap — the Arapaho people were mostly traders; it wasn't their way to take prisoners or trap people, well, not usually. Besides, he knew he could well take care of himself if there was a fight up ahead.

But his first thought was for Bear. If

an Indian had come looking for him, then Bear must have sent him somehow, so it must be bad. Bear could usually tend to his own wounds, and any that might have needed more attention than that, well, Cade couldn't think of a time when Bear hadn't tended to his own wounds, even stitching up quite deep gashes, aided only by large slugs of moonshine, so this must be serious.

The two riders didn't speak, they couldn't, they just urged their animals into the fastest gallop they could sustain, knowing that, where there were trees, there was water. They'd drink their fill just as soon as they reached their target.

As the two men drew closer to the trees, their pace slowed. When they entered the treeline they both dismounted swiftly. Cade motioned to Pack Rat to go ahead with his pony, and he followed closely with Sky. As they moved carefully through the trees, they could hear the sound of a soft, slow drumbeat. Cade's sharp ears also picked out the sound of a woman's voice, chanting softly in time to the beats.

As they drew closer to the sound, Be-xoo-kuu held up a hand to stop them. He led his pony down to a small stream, and let it drink its fill. Cade gave Sky his head to do likewise. When the men were satisfied that their animals had sated their thirst, they led them over to the trees, and tied them to a low branch.

Going forward on foot behind Pack Rat, Cade could hear the drum and the chanting growing louder now. As they reached the small clearing, Cade instantly took in the shape of Bear, lying flat out on the ground, close by a small fire. Blood was spread in patches everywhere around the clearing. He could see, though, that Bear was still breathing. Cade knelt down beside him, and grabbed his hand.

'I'm here, old man, it's me, it's Cade. What the hell's happened here, Bear?'

His only answer was a low groan. Bear's eyelids flickered a little but didn't open. Cade squeezed his hand.

'Bear, c'mon, partner, I'm here now. Be-xoo-kuu found me, he bought me here, talk to me, old man, talk to me. Please.'

Bear made a feeble attempt to squeeze Cade's hand, but the movement was so weak as to be hardly noticeable. Cade grabbed the old man, and held him close to his chest. This man was his best friend, the closest thing to a father he'd ever had, and now he could be dying. Cade couldn't let that happen. Hot tears ran down his cheeks.

'Bear, c'mon, you old bastard, stay with me, I'll look after you — we'll look after you. You'll be fine. C'mon, old man.'

Bear groaned. Cade let him slowly back down to the ground. The drumbeat was still going on, and the woman was still chanting softly, somewhere. Looking round the clearing, Cade's eyes fell on the slim figure of a young woman, seated beneath a nearby tree, slowly beating a small skin-covered drum. She stopped her drumming, and looked up as his gaze landed on her. Cade was knocked for six. Indian she was, in dress and hairstyle, with a fringed buckskin dress and beaded headband, holding back two waist-length black braids, but she was pale, with high cheekbones, and almond-shaped, wide, pale-blue eyes. Her chanting had stopped when she realized Cade was watching her so closely. He knew he had never seen anything as beautiful as her. He stared.

'Cade — Wo-xuu?' Pack Rat touched his shoulder, and pointed at Bear, frowning, obviously asking if Cade could do anything for Bear. He felt completely helpless.

'I — I — don't know.'

He shrugged his shoulders and shook his head. He moved the old man's hand and pulled his thick fur jacket to one side. His clothes were ripped and torn and covered in blood. The wound in his side was deep, wide and still bleeding. It was very recent. It had been packed with some sort of moss, Cade reckoned that Pack Rat had tried to help, or this beautiful Native girl, who was now so quiet, and looking at him with those wide, disconcertingly blue eyes.

'I can't do anything at all here. We need to get him into Kicking Horse — it's closest, and there's a doctor there who might be able to fix him. What happened to the animal?'

Then he felt stupid; these Natives couldn't understand what he was saying. It was good that they were obviously friends of Bear's, and he must have told them where to find him, but Bear could probably speak their lingo fluently. Cade only had a few words, and with Bear in this state, there was no translator to let them know what he was going to do. He didn't want them to think he was a threat. A soft voice made him turn quickly.

'Mr Cade? Kicking Horse, long ride

from here. If I pad wound well, you help Be-xoo-kuu build strong travois, and we travel fast, we might then save him. If your doctor will help.'

She spoke almost perfect English. A breed then for sure, but what was she doing here? Of course, she must be Pack Rat's wife. OK. He shook his head to clear it.

'Yeah, the doc will help.'

'But he will need your money, we do not have money, how can he help?'

She was crying silently now. Cade thought fast.

'Look, I know someone who owes me a favour. He has money, much money. He'll pay off the doctor for me — he promised me he'd help me if I needed it. I'm sure he'll do this for me.'

'For us,' she retorted firmly, looking him right in the eyes. 'We go with you, if he is going to die, I need to be near.'

'Why do you need to be near, Miss — ?'

'My name is Nii-ehihi, in your words, Little Bird. Wo-xuu, my Father,' she stated matter-of-factly. She knelt beside the old man, and very gently checked the terrible wound, adding some more dried herbs to the moss already there. Cade was speechless.

'I — he never — well, the old coot!! He never told me. I thought he was my friend, and he never told me something like that!'

'Do not be angry with him, Mr Cade, he was only told it three moons ago. My mother would tell no one but her younger sister. She left a skin bag for me to open if she . . . if she . . . would die. There were papers in it. Then . . . Wo-xuu comes to us, and . . . ' she sobbed.

Pack Rat put his arm around her. Yeah, they were married all right.

'OK, let's get this travois together, c'mon.'

She and Bear could explain it all later, if Bear lived that long. Right now, there was no more time to waste. Cade spotted Bear's axe lying covered in blood, on the ground beside him, and picked it up. He started looking for the right sort of branches to make the sides and the crossbars. Pack Rat was ahead of him, and had his own tomahawk out, chopping a stout branch from a nearby tree. Cade went to start chopping at another one that he thought looked about right, when a call stopped him. Pack Rat chattered something, and pointed to a different tree. The girl spoke.

'He says that is not strong for travois, the other tree is better.'

Cade obeyed, and the two men, red and white, worked side by side, chopping, trimming, and tying the triangular framework together. The girl had been plaiting grasses, and she wasted no time in threading and tying them to the framework. She threw a deerskin over the framework, and stepped back to check it.

'Strong, good,' she said quietly, casting a sideways glance at Cade. Then she started to pile the drum, and other belongings, which were scattered around the glade into a blanket, tying it together with a thong.

Pack Rat kicked the fire out, making sure there were no stray ashes left behind, and looked at Cade. Smiling, he pointed at the travois. 'Cade, good.'

Cade replied, 'Be-xoo-kuu, good.' The two men shook hands.

Cade turned to the girl, 'Is Bear — your father — is he fit to travel now?'

'I have packed the wound well and given him my medicine to last to the doctor. I hope he will travel well. Be-xoo-kuu will fetch pony now.'

She spoke to the warrior in their own language and he ran off into the trees. Moments later, he came back, leading his own pony and Sky. He and the girl quickly harnessed, and strapped the travois on to the pony as Cade watched. The girl moved with a sinuous grace that left him speechless.

As soon as he knew the travois was ready, Cade gently lifted Bear, and placed him on the framework. The old trapper groaned softly. Cade held on to him tightly, and whispered in his ear.

'You hold on in there, old man, hold on for me, and for your . . . your daughter. We've got to have a long talk about that, you old coot. Don't you dare go dyin' on me till you've told me that particular tale. Just hold on in there, Bear.'

He placed the injured man central on the travois. The girl handed him a blanket and he covered Bear up, then took off his own coat, and threw that over the top of the blanket — Bear had to be kept warm. The girl strapped her bundle on to the back of the pony and spoke to the man, who nodded his head at Cade, and they all moved off slowly through the trees, walking, and leading the horses along the winding path.

Cade knew that, when they reached the plain, they'd really have to get a move on or Bear would have no real chance, judging by what he'd seen of the wound. But there were three of them walking, and only two horses; the Indian pony was heavily loaded, so no one could ride it. The girl could ride double on Sky with Cade, but what would Pack Rat do? Bear's mules were nowhere in sight, so they couldn't make use of them. They soon reached the end of the treeline. The two Indians were talking together heatedly. The girl turned to Cade.

'Mr Cade, is it right in your laws that I am permitted to ride on your animal with you?'

'Sure you can, under these circumstances, and you can hold on to the pony's lead rein, but what will Be-xoo-koo do?'

'Oh, he will run alongside.' Her comment was matter-of-fact.

Cade shook his head. It was a long way — how could this guy run that far? But then he knew that Indians were a damn sight tougher than most white men he knew, so maybe this one would be able to do just that.

'Let's go then.'

He mounted Sky, and held out his hand for the girl to mount. She grabbed his hand and swung easily and lightly up behind him, holding onto the pony's rope. Cade kicked Sky into a trot. He could feel the warmth of the girl so close behind him, and hear and feel her soft breathing in his ear.

The warrior was trotting alongside of them at a steady pace, keeping up well. Cade couldn't kick Sky into a headlong gallop — he was loaded, and the other pony was even more so — but he pushed on as fast as he could, the Indian keeping right alongside of them, and to Cade's eyes, he didn't even look to be panting. Soon, the outline of the town came into view.

'Close now, good,' Little Bird whispered.

Then they spotted a group of riders heading towards them. Not good. The last thing they needed was to have to stop now. But the riders were headed directly for them, and Cade knew there was absolutely no chance of avoiding them. As the two groups drew closer, Cade realized that trouble was only moments away. He recognized the portly figure of Frank Lee, the leader of the bunch of kids that Cade had rescued George Phillips from. He was riding with around six other young men. Cade whispered back over his shoulder.

'Tell Be-xoo-kuu to be ready for a fight; these guys are a bad lot.'

Little Bird spoke to the man. Cade saw his muscles tighten and his hand go to the tomahawk at his belt. He just hoped that they'd be able to get through the group, and on into the town quickly enough to save Bear. The others drew closer, and Cade saw that Frank Lee had made him out at last. The boy spoke to the others.

'Well lookee here, we got ourselves a raidin' party, boys. Can't let them get into town, who knows what they might do, huh?'

Cade sighed. Not again, this boy hadn't learned his lesson after all.

'Look, Lee, the old man's my friend,

he's hurt bad, we need to get to the doc.'

'He an Injun too? Sure looks like it, and what're you doin' ridin with Injuns anyway? I knew you were a wrong 'un when we met last time, just didn't know how wrong you were. She your squaw?'

Be-xoo-kuu was standing silently, looking at the small group, Cade knew he was collecting his strength, and quietly judging their strengths and weaknesses: he worked the same way Cade did.

'No, Lee, my friend's not an Indian, and she's not my squaw, she's my friend, they all are. But you wouldn't know about friends, would you? You're just a bully. All the boys who ride with you only do it because they're scared of what you'll do to them. Look, kid, remember what happened last time we met? You don't want it to happen again, now do you?'

He felt Little Bird squeeze his arm, he knew she was right — he shouldn't be provoking them — but his anger was growing fast. Bear, his best and oldest friend, his only family, could be dying, and this gang of thugs were making it impossible for him to get the old man into town. He wasn't happy, and the anger was churning wildly inside him. Lee drew his gun, and most of the others followed suit. Cade and his friends now had five Colts pointed at them, at almost point-blank range.

'Get down off of there, Cade, and get that woman down too. We'll have fun with her later. Pete, you keep her covered. Tell the savage to put his hands behind his back, Cade. Tom, you get down and tie that damn Injun up.'

'Why me?'

'Shut the hell up and do as I say.'

Tom dismounted as Cade helped Little Bird to dismount and got down himself. They mustn't know she could speak English, so as he lifted her down, he put his lips close to her ear and whispered, 'Please, say nothing,' She nodded gently and squeezed his arm again. He turned back to face the group of boys.

'Lee, come on, kid, I don't speak their language well enough to tell him that. Suppose you give it a try,' Cade smiled.

'You must be able to, you're ridin' with 'em!'

'Yeah, but it's the old man there who's the interpreter. They're his friends, not mine.'

'Tom, you tell the redskin to put his hands behind his back,' Lee ordered, waving his gun at his companion.

'I don't speak Injun!'

'Well show him then!'

Lee had his gun on Pack Rat; one boy was covering the girl, and the rest were watching either Cade or the Indian. Tom stood in front of Pack Rat and mimed him putting his hands behind his back. The Indian looked down at him and smiled, but didn't move.

'He won't do it, Frank.'

'Well you just bloody well make him, then.'

The boy pulled out his gun, and shoved it in Be-xoo-kuu's face.

'Hands. You. Hands behind back!' he shouted.

Nothing, the Indian didn't even blink when the gun almost touched his nose. Frank was getting sick of this by now.

'Jamie, you get down and make the red bastard do it. Pistol whip him if you have to. Don, you go and tie the white Injun up.'

The two boys dismounted. That was better, three on the ground now, and Cade's anger was threatening to explode. Bear was dying here, and these idiots were playing games. They didn't know what they were messing with.

'Come on, get them tied, they can both watch while we play with the girl.'

The boy's laugh froze Cade's blood; he wasn't about to let any harm come to Little Bird.

As the boy named Don drew closer, Cade began to tense up. He glanced across at Pack Rat, who quickly returned his look, and in that very instant, even without a common language, they both knew what had to be done.

At the same moment, Cade grabbed Don's arm and whipped him off his feet, while Pack Rat drew his tomahawk, threw it at one of the boys still on his horse, hitting him square in the middle of his chest and knocking him backwards from his horse, then grabbed one of the arms of each of the boys standing, blinking, close to him. Swiftly then, he pulled them towards one another, they collided, guns firing harmlessly into the air. Pack Rat drew his knife and swiftly dispensed with his two opponents. One of the remaining boys quickly turned his horse, and galloped off, with Pack Rat in close pursuit.

Meantime, seeing what was happening, Cade also used his knife, finishing off Don in an instant. As he turned from his prey, he heard a noise and looked round. Frank Lee had dismounted with his other henchman and grabbed Little Bird. They had her on the ground; she was struggling against them like a landed trout, kicking and biting, but in almost complete silence. Cade didn't dare to shoot just in case he hit the girl, so he ran over to them and grabbed the two boys, pulling them both up from the squirming girl by the scruffs of their necks, helped somewhat by Little Bird viciously kicking them from her as he heaved them off.

The fight that ensued was fierce and bloody; Cade against the two younger men, they stood no chance. He pulled no punches. He had Frank Lee in a strangle hold, and when the other boy went to draw his gun, Little Bird launched herself at him, and they both ended up in a heap, struggling and fighting on the floor. The gun went off. Cade and Lee continued to wrestle it out, until Lee managed to draw his knife.

'Cade!'

Little Bird's call drew his attention to the danger. He grabbed the boy's wrist and twisted hard, breaking bones. Lee screamed in pain. Cade turned the knife towards the boy and plunged it into his chest, to the hilt. As the boy fell to the floor, Cade turned to go and help Little Bird, but she was standing over the body of the boy who lay at her feet with his neck broken, the gun lying beside his body. At that moment Pack Rat rode up to them on the horse of the boy who he had been chasing. His hands and chest were covered in blood.

Little Bird smiled up at Pack Rat — Cade's heart did a back flip, when he saw that smile — then she turned and spoke softly to him.

'Cade, we have more horses now, we can get to town faster. This is good, come.'

She swung quickly up onto one of the other horses and, pulling the pony with the travois, she headed for town as fast as the horses could go with the load, Be-xoo-kuu following. Cade swiftly re-mounted Sky and headed after them, catching them up and pulling in alongside them.

'Little Bird, let me go in front with Bear. I will speak to the doctor. If they see you and Be-xoo-kuu with him, well, they might just think it was you who hurt him.'

'NO! I take him in, he is my father. Show me this doctor.'

Cade wasn't about to waste his time arguing with her, he urged Sky on and soon they were at the doctor's surgery. The few people who were around looked oddly at them, but Cade leaped off Sky, ran to the travois, scooped up Bear in his arms and with Little Bird close on his heels, entered the surgery.

The nurse tried to stop them from going into the doctor, but Cade just pushed past her with Little Bird close at his back, and walked into the surgery. The doctor was tending to an elderly man, bandaging his arm, and looked up, surprised at the sudden interruption of his work.

'I'm sorry, Doctor, I couldn't stop

them,' the nurse called.

'Doc, I'm real sorry, this here man's been mauled by a bear, it's bad. Little Bird did what she could, but we need your help now. Can you fix him?'

The doctor finished up, and dismissed the elderly man, who left the room with the nurse, then the doctor looked at the old man in Cade's arms.

'Put him on the table, I'll take a look,' he said coldly.

Cade laid his friend gently down, and drew back his jacket, exposing the wound. The doctor examined it as best he could through the ripped and bloodied clothes, and whistled under his breath.

'Look, we need to get his clothes off first, and this stuff out of the wound before I can tell if I can save him. I won't lie to you, though, he's hurt really bad.'

He and Cade spent some moments moving Bear about, and taking off his clothes, dropping them to the floor, where Little Bird collected them into a pile in the corner, and sat on them, watching with those wide, pale-blue, tear-filled eyes. Bear's old body was bony and dirty, covered in dark bruises, and big old scars, and right in the middle of it all, there was a gaping wound in his side, oozing blood and packed up with moss and grass.

The doctor called, 'Nurse! Close the door for the day, and come in here, I need help.'

'What can I do?' said Cade.

'Well you can start by thinking how you're going to pay for this treatment, Mr Cade. It'll take some time to fix this up and if he lives through it, it'll take a good long time before I'd let him out of my care. It won't come cheap.'

The doctor looked up at him across Bear's broken body, and his eyes were serious.

'Understand, though, that even with my help, he might not pull through — this is real bad.'

'We know that, sir. Look, I'm goin' to go sort out the money. Little Bird here, she speaks good English. She's his daughter, she'll help if you need an extra pair of hands, and her husband is outside. He doesn't speak English but if you need any more help tell her, she'll go get him.'

He turned to Little Bird, 'I'll be back very soon, pray for him.' He turned on his heels, not hearing her soft reply as he left the surgery and jumped on to Sky.

He knew where he had to go. And he headed there with speed.

9

George Phillips was sitting on his veranda, watching, as his men got on with the general running of the ranch, when his eye was taken by a plume of dust heading his way, coming from the town of Kicking Horse. He called out to the nearest two hands.

'Joe, Red, here. Hang around, see what gives — someone coming this way, fast.'

He motioned towards the dust cloud and the two men loosened the guns in their holsters, ready for whatever might be headed their way. As the cloud of dust drew closer, they could see it was a lone rider, moving fast. When he was close enough, Phillips thought he recognized the man on the big paint. As he pulled to a skidding halt in front of the house and leaped from his horse, Phillips held up his hand to stop his men drawing their guns.

'It's OK boys, I know this man, he's the one who rescued my Esme, and put Gerrard behind bars. I'll be fine with him. Get on with your work.'

The men reluctantly withdrew, keeping a surreptitious eye on their boss, just in case there was trouble. Cade strode over to Phillips, who stood, and held out his hand.

'Jed, you're always welcome here, you know that, but you're in a pretty damn hurry. What's wrong?'

Cade took his hand in a firm grip, but Phillips could feel the big man shaking.

'Y'remember, George, you once said if'n there was anything you could do for me . . . ?'

'Sure I remember, and you better damn well know that I meant it. Anything, just name it.' He saw the hesitation in the other man's face.

'Jed, you brought me back my little girl, and to me she's more precious than any gold or diamonds. If I can ever repay you for that gift I most certainly will, whatever it might cost.'

'That's it, George, it will cost, that's why I don't really like to ask, but it's not for me — '

'Come, sit, tell me all about it.'

He led Cade to the bench on the veranda, and the two men sat side by side, Phillips waiting patiently until Cade pulled up the courage to tell him. He knew the man was normally outspoken, and wondered at the hesitation. But once Cade started to tell the story, Phillips realized just what that old man must mean to him, probably about as much as Esme meant to him.

'Red! Saddle my horse, I'm going into town with Mr Cade here.'

Within minutes the two men were riding back into Kicking Horse. At the surgery, they dismounted and tied their animals to the hitching rail. Cade spotted Pack Rat sitting near by and went over to him.

'Be-xoo-kuu? What's happening? Wo-xuu?'

The Indian shrugged his shoulders,

and nodded his head towards the surgery, saying something that Cade couldn't make out. He went then with Phillips into the building, and they were met by the nurse. There was blood on her apron and hands.

'Oh hello, Mr Phillips, Mr Cade.'

'How's Bear, is he gonna be OK?'

'Too soon to say just yet. Doctor's still working on him; it was a very bad wound. It'll be some time yet so why don't you sit here and wait a while. I'll let you know just as soon as Doctor can tell me anything.'

Cade took off his hat, and went slowly over to sit on one of the hard wooden seats.

'Mr Phillips, what brings you here? Are you unwell?' asked the nurse.

'Nope, Nancy, I'm just fine. I'm with Mr Cade here. Tell the doc to give the old man the very best care he can, no expense to be spared. I'm picking up the tab for this.'

The nurse looked from him to Cade and back again, a puzzled frown on her stern features. Then she picked up some instruments from a small glass-fronted cabinet, turned, and headed back to the consulting room, which was now doubling as an operating theatre. As she opened the door, Cade went to rise. Phillips stopped him.

'No Jed, too many people in there will just crowd the doc, and he won't be able to do his job. Let's just sit and wait. Your friend will be fine, I'm sure. Doc Barton is one of the best, and now he knows I'm paying, your friend will get the best care possible. Relax a while, Nancy'll come out when there's any news.'

They sat on the hard chairs, silently. Cade shuffled on his seat, embarrassed.

'I really don't know how to thank you, George.'

'Hey, he's not out of the woods yet by the sound of it. Thank me if he makes it.'

'It means a hell of a lot. You know — '

'As what you did for my Esme back

there meant to me, Jed, so now we're quits, huh?' Phillips squeezed Cade's arm. Some time later, the door opened. Both men stood up; the Indian girl came out, dried blood on her hands, tears on her cheeks. Cade leaped to his feet.

'Little Bird, how is he?' he asked hesitantly.

She rushed forward, and grabbed hold of him, falling into his arms. He held on to her tightly, knowing now just how much Bear meant to her, as well as to him.

'Oh, Cade, he will be well, a long time to heal, but he will be well. Thank you so much.'

Phillips watched with interest as the two clung to one another.

'George Phillips, this is my friend Bear's daughter, Little Bird. Little Bird, this man is paying the money to the doctor for Bear's medicine and care.'

She looked up at the older man, puzzled.

'Why are you paying the money? I

thank you very much, but why is this? You do not know my father.'

'No, miss, I don't, but Mr Cade here, he rescued my own daughter from a vicious band of outlaws who had stolen her away from me. He went in there single-handed, killed them all and brought my daughter safely home. He would take nothing from me in return for that, so I told him, if he ever needed anything, no matter what, I would help him. So now, it's my turn to help him.'

'Hey, I didn't kill 'em all, George,' Cade said almost bashfully.

'Nigh on, but you did give me back my little girl, Cade. This is my thanks to you for that very precious gift.'

He looked down at the Indian girl, she was real pretty and he could see how Cade would have fallen for her. The wide, pale-blue, eyes would have given away the fact that she was a breed, even if Cade hadn't said she was the old trapper's daughter. She'd look mighty pretty in one of Esme's gowns, he'd bet.

The nurse came out, giving them almost the same message as Little Bird had. Then she left and headed off down the main street on an errand. The men sat down to wait for the Doctor to finish. Little Bird went to tell Be-xoo-kuu what was going on.

'She sure is a pretty little thing, Cade. I see now why you weren't interested in my Esme.'

'No, George, that's not how it is. The Indian I spoke to out there, he's her husband. I only met her today. But, well, maybe if'n I'd met her earlier, maybe . . . ' his voice trailed away.

Phillips smiled, he knew love sick when he saw it, and he could see that Cade, Crazy Man Cade, the cold killing machine, was about as besotted with the little Indian girl as a man could get. Maybe Cade was trying to convince himself against it, but it was plain for just about everyone, even a blind man to see. The big man fair lit up when the girl was around. Little Bird came back into the surgery and sat beside Cade silently. Phillips spoke, breaking the silence, and making the girl jump.

'Little Bird, have you told your husband what's happening with your father?'

She looked round at him, puzzled.

'My — my husband? I am a maiden, unmarried, sir.'

She lowered her eyes, embarrassed.

'I'm so sorry, I do apologise, miss, but we thought that the man outside, well, we sort of thought he was your husband.' He saw Cade looking at him sheepishly, and smiled. 'Well that's what Cade told me, anyway.'

She looked up at Cade.

'Who tells you I am married to Be-xoo-kuu? Not Wo-xuu?'

It was Cade's turn to be embarrassed now.

'No, not Wo-xuu. I saw you both together, you are very . . . close. I thought — I apologize Little Bird, I thought — '

'Be-xoo-kuu is my brother,' she

200

laughed, and Cade's heart fluttered at the sound. 'True, we are close, we have same mother. His father died, Wo-xuu came, and took his mother to wife, I was born. Wo-xuu, he has feet filled with fire ants, cannot stay in one place. Before I came, he left my mother, she never took another man, and never spoke, but to her sister, about him.'

She stopped, and looked at the ground, gathering her thoughts.

'We knew he was white, because of my eyes, but not who. Twelve moons ago, my mother died. She left me her skin bag. In it, with other things, I find two papers; one say she and Wo-xuu were married in Mexico, and one say I am born with his name. I did not know who my father was, my mother is dead, so Be-xoo-kuu is my guardian. Then, three moons ago, Wo-xuu came, and he found me. We talk, he said who I am, stayed for a while, then left again, asked Be-xoo-kuu to look after me.'

She began to cry, and Cade put his arm around her. Feeling her small, slender body so close made his pulse race. Her hair was cool, and silken soft beneath his cheek; she smelled of meadow flowers, cool river water, and wild honey. He felt warm, the relief he felt surprised him greatly. She was unmarried — maybe he stood a chance. Chance? Chance for what? He was concerned for Bear, so why was he also thinking about this beautiful Native girl? No, she wasn't really Native, she was breed, she was Bear's daughter, after all. Hell, this was confusing. He'd have to have words with them both when Bear was back on his feet again, get the whole story, from both sides.

It took a few days before Bear regained consciousness and was able to speak. The Indians had made a small camp just outside of town, and during that time, either Little Bird or Cade visited with Bear each day, sitting beside his bed for hours at a time, while a fever raged through his ravaged body, and he tossed and turned, rambled and muttered in several languages.

One morning, though, as Cade entered the small room to take his turn sitting with the old man, Bear looked up at him as he approached the bed and spoke in a weak, croaking voice.

'Hell, kid, didn't think I'd ever be seein' your ugly face again.'

'Bear! You're awake! I'll get the doctor.'

He made to leave, almost tripping over his own feet in his hurry.

'S' all right, he's been in to me already, says I'm doin' just fine now. How long was I out for, kid?'

'Almost a week now.'

Cade sat beside him, his heart pumping. Bear was alive and would be fine. Thank any of the gods that might be looking down. He took hold of the old-timer's hand. Bear squeezed his fingers. Cade felt a tear run down his cheek.

'We didn't think you were gonna make it, old man.'

'Who we?'

Bear frowned, tried to sit up and

groaned, lying back against the pillows.

'Doc didn't tell you? I had plenty of help in getting you here. A Pack Rat and a Little Bird helped!'

Bear managed a smile. 'Be-xoo-kuu and Little Bird? I had a feelin' they were somewhere around. How you all been getting on together?'

'Real fine, real fine. He's a tough one, that Pack Rat, and Little Bird . . . Hey, old man, why didn't you tell me about her?'

'Only found out a little while ago myself. She's a sweet one, looks just like her mom, but with my eyes.'

'That's what you were tryin' to tell me that night when we made camp together? Why didn't you finish up telling me?'

'Guess I didn't think the time was right, huh?'

'Would there ever have been a right time, old man?'

He squeezed Bear's hand, and smiled down at his grizzled friend. He'd never seen him look so bad, but Doc said he was improving, and he certainly looked better than he had on the day he'd come in here.

'Did you kill the bear? I didn't see its body in the clearing.'

'Nope. Must be gettin' old, kid, just wounded it, that's why it turned like it did. It was just about the biggest I'd ever seen, after the one whose tooth you've got, of course. He was a whopper. I just made a mistake, thought he was off guard, but he wasn't. Half my best knife's still buried in his chest. Hope for his sake that he died of his wounds, elsewise — '

Cade was suddenly alert.

'Hell, Bear, if it's just wounded, it'll be going crazy out there. Could even find its way to a cabin, or even the town and kill somebody. Or if'n anyone goes in there for any reason . . . '

They looked at one another, both knowing that a wounded bear was just about the deadliest creature on this earth.

'I gotta go and find it and make sure

it's dead so it can't do any more damage to anyone.'

'No, kid! It could just as easy kill you. I wounded it pretty well. After I shot it, it fell, but then it got back up and came at me like a bullet. I got another round into it before it grabbed me, then I stuck it with my knife, real deep in its chest, while it had a hold of me. Then it picked me up and bloody well shook me like an old hound dog with a rat.'

He grinned crookedly.

'When I woke up, it was gone. I lay there for quite a while before Little Bird and Be-xoo-kuu found me. Pure coincidence they were there at that time, although they wouldn't say that. They'd be sayin' that it was all the doin' of Wakan-Tonka, who guided them to me when I was most in need.'

'Well, maybe it was but whatever it was that guided them there, they saved you. But I gotta go see if that bear is dead, old man, you do know that?'

'Guess so, someone has to. I'm sorry, Cade, I . . . '

He began to drift off to sleep. Cade left him then, and went out to where Little Bird was sitting with Be-xoo-kuu, stirring a pot of rice over the fire.

'He's regained consciousness, er — woken up, but he's tired, and he's going back to sleep. Little Bird, you go in and sit with him, so he sees you when he wakes up again.'

She jumped up, and grabbed hold of him like a drowning man to a log.

'Thank you, Mr Cade. Thank you for helping him.'

She ran off to sit with her father leaving Cade to sit beside Pack Rat. They were silent for a long while, each man lost in his own thoughts. The passers-by didn't stare much now, in the past week they'd kind of got used to seeing a couple of Indians around town; it wasn't so much of a novelty any more. The doctor came out then, and walked over to them, nodding his head at the Indian.

'Mr Cade, your friend is making a pretty good recovery, I'm surprised at his tenacity. Those wounds would have killed even a much younger man, but the girl did a very good job of patching him up and easing the pain until he got here. If it hadn't been for her, and for your swiftness in getting him to me, the outcome would have been very different. George Phillips came by yesterday, and paid up the bill. He thinks very highly of you, Mr Cade. The old man will need to stay in the infirmary, probably for another couple of weeks, for the wound to mend completely, and George has paid for that too. He's a very generous man.'

'He is that,' agreed Cade, 'more than generous. Thank you for taking such good care of old Bear, Doc, it means a lot.'

The men shook hands, and the doctor returned to his surgery. Cade followed and spoke to Little Bird, telling her he was going to see Phillips.

He didn't want her to know about the injured bear. He rode on out to the Phillips ranch first, though; he had to thank the man for what he'd done, see if there was any way he could repay the other man's generosity. George had more than repaid him for rescuing his daughter. He was a little concerned, though, that Esme might just try and waylay him again. He knew that she was definitely on the lookout for a husband, but he also knew he wasn't going to be it.

There was no one on the veranda as he approached, no horses at the rail. He looked around; the place looked almost deserted, but he could see the cattle, so he knew there must be someone about. He dismounted, hitched up Sky and walked up the steps towards the front door.

'That's far enough, mister.'

Cade swung round; a figure had appeared round the corner of the house, with two guns drawn and ready. Cade recognized him as one of the men who'd been swarming round Esme at the party. Tall, slim, blond-haired, short beard and cocksure of himself. With both guns aimed at Cade, and ready to fire.

'Just here to pay my respects to Mr Phillips and his girl,' said Cade, eyeing the man.

'Yeah? Well you just take your respects and ride back the way you came, go on.'

The blond man gestured with one of the guns.

'Who are you? Can you speak for Mr Phillips? Tell him I'm here, Cade's the name, he knows me.'

'Yeah, and so do I. Tryin' to worm your way into the family. Miss Esme wouldn't be takin' up with a loser like you, so get!'

Cade felt the anger stirring. Who in the hell did this guy think he was? Stopping him from going in to see Phillips? He wasn't the foreman, Cade had met the foreman, so who was he?

'Look, I ain't got no argument with

you, mister. Just put your guns away and tell George I'm here.'

'George, is it? Cozyin' up to him, eh, just to get close to Miss Esme? Well she don't want to see you, and neither does 'George', so suppose you just turn right round and clear off, eh, before I fill you full of lead.'

Cade's hands itched to draw on the man, but he knew damn well his guns wouldn't clear their holsters before the other man could shoot. His irons were already in his hands, and he was close enough not to miss. Cade guessed that, if he turned his back on this guy, he could end up shot in it, so he stood still, looking the man up and down with cold, hard eyes.

'Who gave you permission to be the guard dog then?'

'I don't need nobody's permission. This'll soon be my place, then losers like you'll be shot dead at the gate.'

The man smiled broadly, a gold tooth flashing. Cade went cold: what had this guy done to the family? Where were

George and Esme Phillips? He needed to find out, but if he shouted, he'd most likely get shot anyway. Just then, as if at a signal, the door opened. The guy with the guns holstered them fast. Conchita smiled weakly at Cade.

'Mr Cade, I will tell Mr Phillips you are here — we thought we heard a horse come in. Please wait here.'

She made to turn and go indoors. Cade was right behind her, and blocked her from closing it. He smiled down at her.

'Thank you, Conchita. Yes, I'll wait in the hall.'

She looked Cade up and down and made to speak, and then seeing the other man standing so close behind him, silently stepped to one side to allow Cade to pass, and closed the door behind them, leaving the other man staring angrily at the closing door. She disappeared into one of the rooms, and moments later George Phillips came out to greet him with a broad smile, hand outstretched.

'Jed! Great to see you again. How're you doing?'

'I'm just dandy, George, thanks. How's about you, and Miss Esme?'

The older man's eyes clouded over as they shook hands warmly, and he guided Cade into the library, closing the heavy door behind him, and offering Cade a seat and a cheroot. He took one himself, and lit them both, then sat at his large desk, and leaned heavily on it. It was a while before he spoke. Cade didn't want to interrupt him, so he just sat quietly, waiting.

'Esme is a problem, Jed. She had her sights fair set on you, and when you left, she cried for two days, then pulled herself together, and started making eyes at all the hands. She was responsible for a few fights and I had to run one man off my land when Conchita caught him in Esme's room.'

He sighed deeply. 'She's played them off against one another, and finally settled on Burton out there, as the guy she wanted to marry. I tried to warn her

213

off him, I know he's a wrong'un, but she'll have none of it. And now he's going round telling all and sundry that he's going to marry her, and take over the ranch from me. I can't face up to him in a gun battle, and he's a cruel man. He's hit Conchita more than once.'

'Has he hit Esme? Or you?'

Cade was fuming at the mere thought.

'Not yet, but I know he's come close, I've seen the signs, and he lords it over the other hands. I've had to make him foreman.'

'Why?' Cade was incredulous.

'It was the old foreman who was caught in Esme's room. I needed to replace him and Burton cosied up to me and volunteered, so I passed it on to him. That was just before I realized what a snake he really is.'

Cade leaped up, angry as hell.

'For god's sake, George, you gotta get rid of him, or you and your daughter will die, and he'll own the ranch. You've been here for years; it was your folks' place. Yeah?'

Phillips nodded slowly, Cade could see he was weary.

'We'll get rid of him, George.'

'How're you going to do that, Jed? No I don't want you to answer that, I know you have your own way of working. And the less I know about that the better, eh? Esme'll be devastated; she'll never forgive me — us — if he dies.'

'She'd be more devastated if'n she married him and then he killed you, and beat her.'

Phillips nodded. 'Yes, but what will I tell her? She means the world to me, you know that, and I don't want to hurt her. Killing Burton will hurt her terribly.'

'She must know the sort of man he is?'

'I don't know, she won't talk to me any more, and she just shouts at Conchita all the time these days. It's not like her at all.'

'Will you allow me to talk to her?'

'Yes of course, anything to help her see sense.'

'Well I don't know if I'll be able to do that, but I'll damn well try, and then I'll get rid of Burton for you.'

Phillips called for Conchita and asked her to bring Esme to them. Moments later the two women returned. Cade was shocked at what he saw: she was stick-thin; her beautiful hair was dull and her clothes were hanging off her. Esme's eyes were harder than he remembered, and she stared at him as if he was dirt. She looked him up and down contemptuously.

'What do you want, Cade?'

She almost spat the question out.

'Just checking that you were feelin' OK, Miss Esme, is all.'

'Yeah? Well you've checked, now go. No one asked you to come poking your Indian-loving nose in. Or did you call him over, Pa?'

She whirled round to face her father, who almost shrank beneath her fiery stare.

'No, Esme, I didn't call him. Mr Cade just came to see how we were, out of the goodness of his heart.'

'Goodness? Goodness? Huh! Nobody's got any goodness in their hearts. Clear out, Cade, or I'll get Burton to see you off our property.'

'Es!' Her father gasped.

'Oh shut up!'

She turned, and flounced towards the door. Cade grabbed her arm as she drew close to him, and almost pulled her off her feet. She squealed and glared at him.

'Remove your hand, now!'

She tried to pull away, but Cade held her hard.

'Miss Esme, this isn't you, you know how much your poor father cares for you. Look what you're doin' to him. Why in the hell are you behaving like this? Burton's poisoning your mind, can't you see that?'

'I'll have you know, I'm going to marry Peter Burton, and then this ranch will be ours, and then losers like you will be shot if you dare come here again. Now go!'

She jerked herself free from his grip and ran from the library to the front door, flinging it open and running straight into the arms of Burton. Cade watched carefully as the man wrapped his arms around the sobbing girl, and looked over her head, leering at the two men who had followed closely behind her.

'You'll be OK now, Esme dear. What did they do to you?'

'He hurt me.'

She sobbed. Cade knew that this wasn't the same girl he'd rescued; something had changed her, and in a very short time.

'I knew you were trouble, mister, the minute you rode in here. Now you've hurt my fiancée, and I won't stand for that. Get out of here, and if'n I see you a mile from here any time soon, you're dead.'

Burton's voice was hard as granite. Cade slowly stepped towards his horse, all the time keeping an eye on the man who held on to the girl. He could see that he was holding her tighter than was needed; she was crying and trying to get free, but Burton kept pulling her close to him. Clever, he knew Cade wouldn't dare to shoot for fear of hurting the girl. As Cade mounted Sky, he saw Phillips looking at him — there was raw fear in his eyes. Burton was holding Esme in a vice-like grip, and she was struggling against him now.

'Keep still, bitch,' he whispered into her ear.

Cade's sharp ears heard the comment and he saw red. He moved his horse slowly away from the house, looking sideways at the small group as he did so, searching for a way to release Esme from her captor's hold. If he drew his irons now, Burton could kill the girl, or him — maybe if he got lucky, both of them. If he waited and turned his back to ride away, he knew there would be a bullet in his back in moments.

Cade eased Sky to a halt, and sat

looking at Burton. There was real fear in the girl's eyes now. Cade knew that, right at that moment, like a bolt of lightning hitting her, she had finally realized what she was really getting herself into. But how to get her out of it? Rescuing Miss Esme Phillips was becoming quite a habit.

At that moment two of the ranch-hands walked round the side of the house chatting. Burton looked around as they appeared, and, in that split second that his head turned, Cade drew and fired. Burton fell to his knees beside Esme, a single hole in his head. As he dropped, face down in the dust, the other two hands who, for a moment had been frozen still, quickly went to draw their guns.

'Stop, no boys, it's OK!' Phillips shouted quickly.

They replaced their weapons, and hurried over to Burton, looking up in surprise at Cade. He jumped off Sky, and went over to Esme, who had crumpled to the ground in a faint.

Burton's blood was splattered across her face and the front of her dress. He picked her up and took her into the house, calling for Conchita.

She led the way to the girl's room, and he placed her on the bed gently. Conchita gasped when she could finally see the condition Esme was in, and looked at Cade with fear in her eyes.

'She's not hurt, Conchita, just fainted — it's Burton's blood. Look after her.'

Cade went back out to where the men were standing over Burton's body, talking. They went quiet when he appeared. Phillips broke the silence; he went over to Cade, and clapped him on the back.

'Boys, this here is Jed Cade. He seems to make a habit of rescuing folk in trouble, and he's rescued Esme twice now, and me too I reckon. You two sort that pile of shit out. Jed, you join me back in the library, we really need to talk.'

They went back into the library as the hands took care of Burton. They sat in silence for a while, puffing on the quality cheroots, then Phillips broke the silence.

'Y'know how grateful I am to you, yet again, Jed?' He smiled.

'George, you've repaid me big time for rescuing Esme, by paying the doc to treat Bear. He means a lot to me; I want nothing else.'

'I reckoned you'd say that. But what if I asked you to take over from Burton as foreman here? Couldn't get one any better than you, as I can see.'

Cade took some time to think about the offer. It meant settling down, regular, solid employment, no more drifting in the wild. But he'd have to see Esme every day, and he doubted if she'd be happy about that.

'I don't think so, George. Thanks for the offer, I do appreciate it, but, I don't think Miss Esme would be too happy with me hangin' around here all the time.'

'Well, I see your point, she did take quite a shine to you, but that was because you'd rescued her from Gerrard's gang. I reckon she'd be fine with it eventually. There's a small cabin goes with the job, away from the bunkhouse, you could move your friend — Bear? — in with you too. Maybe he could help me out in some way?'

'Sounds good, George, but I know old Bear would never settle to a regular life. Ain't no bears round here for him to chase!'

They laughed together, the mood in the house had lightened.

'What're you going to do about that little Indian girl, Jed?'

The question shook Cade and he blinked and choked on the smoke from the cigar. When he'd finished coughing, he looked up into George Phillips' laughing eyes.

'Come on, I'm an old man, I know moonstruck when I see it. Can't tell me I'm wrong.'

'I — er — well, she's breed actually, you know she's Bear's daughter, I told you.'

223

'Well, Jed, breed or full-blood, she's a pretty little thing, and sassy with it. A man could do a lot worse for himself. She'd dress up well in a pretty ball gown. Conchita could do her hair up like Esme's, and with those big blue eyes of hers, no one would know she was part Indian.'

'I don't care if she's full-blood, she ain't gettin' dressed up in no fancy ball gown!' Cade was angry. 'It ain't right. She belongs out there, not in your 'polite society', she'd never fit in. Any more than I would. I reckon you've just made my mind up for me, George, thank you.'

'So you won't be staying around then?'

He smiled at the look on the younger man's face.

'Nope. Anyways, I only came over today to thank you again for what you did for us. Bear's goin' to be fine; needs a few weeks' rest, then I guess he'll be back to his old tricks. I don't remember my pa; Bear's the nearest I've ever had, so what you did, well, I can't say more than thank you, George.'

He reached across and shook hands with Phillips, knowing he had made a real friend.

'More than happy to help. Any time your travels fetch you up this way again, pop in and visit. You, and your friends, I'll be glad to see you, and I'll damn well make sure I'm careful who I hire from now on.'

Cade didn't wait to say goodbye to Esme; he passed his best wishes on through her father, knowing that now they'd both be more careful who they befriended, and then he headed off fast. He had to go and find himself a wounded bear.

10

When he reached the wooded area where he'd found Bear and the Indians, Cade dismounted, and scouted around for tracks. It took him some time to pick out the signs, then his sharp eyes spotted the bear prints. A little further on he could see the lighter imprints of the old trapper's moccasin boots, heading towards the bear prints. He knew that close by, he would come across the spot where the two of them had met. He reached a small clearing, and whistled as he looked around him: this was where the fight had taken place.

There was blood and hair, flattened grass and broken branches everywhere. The ground was churned up and he spotted a dull glint of metal beside a branch. He picked it up; it was Bear's broken knife. The handle was covered in blood and the blade was broken off jaggedly about halfway down. That must have been one hell of a strong animal to break a hunting knife.

Scouting around the scene, Cade saw a deep depression with blood pooled in the centre of it, which looked as though a heavy weight had laid there for some time. Must have been the bear after the old man had stabbed it. That was how come his friend had managed to escape from it's clutches. He soon found the path that the old man had taken, away from the scene of the fight. There were broken branches along the narrow trail, and a hell of a lot of blood. He shook his head.

'Hell, old man, how did you get away from it alive?'

He wandered around looking for the animal's trail. A gap in the trees drew his eye. There were tufts of thick, dark-brown hair caught up on some of the lower branches and large amounts of blood further along the trail. It was badly wounded. It would be very dangerous if it was still alive. He pulled his guns ready as he carried on following the wide, and very obvious trail.

Some time later, he could see that the animal must be weakening; it had sat down here for a while. There was another large flattened patch, with a fair sized pool of blood within it. He reached out and put his fingers in the blood. Still warm. The creature was mortally wounded. It had been bleeding profusely for some time now; chances were it was already dead, but as the blood was still warm, just maybe it was still alive. He stood still, listening, tuning his ears in, searching for any sound which might tell him the whereabouts of the animal.

There. A low, rasping sound, irregular, gruff, bubbling. He followed the sound very carefully. Just ahead he spotted it. A large, dark brown mound, lying draped over the gnarled bole of a fallen tree. Still breathing, but very close to death now. Slowly he drew closer, guns cocked and ready. He cursed a twig that snapped beneath his boot. The animal lifted its huge head slowly and turned to look at him, but made no attempt to get up. Even as he drew closer, it simply growled deep in its throat, a low, bubbling, gurgling, growl, which Cade knew meant that blood was filling up its insides. It curled its lips back from huge teeth, reached up one enormous arm and flexed its claws towards him, still trying to attack even as it lay dying.

Cade stood as close to the creature as he dared. It was huge even when down. He let off two quick rounds and the animal slumped over the tree and went limp, blood pouring from the two large new holes in its head. Cade waited, still standing in the same spot, still holding both Colts. Couldn't be too safe; if it should happen to come back at him, he was ready. When he was certain it was well and truly dead, he holstered the guns and went over to the body.

It took some effort for him to roll the

body off the trunk by himself; it was a huge creature. Its face was scattered with both old and new scars and it looked to Cade as if it was blind in one eye. He rolled it on to its back, spread its four legs as far apart as he could, drew his skinning knife, and went to work on the creature. It was a lot easier to do the job whilst it was still warm. When he'd finished, he was covered in blood and hair, but he had a huge bear pelt, and a pouch full of teeth and claws. He whistled shrilly and, eventually, Sky appeared nearby. Cade curled the skin into a tight roll, tying it with some of the bear's sinews, and heaved it up and across Sky's broad quarters. Even the pelt was heavy.

As he skinned the animal he had seen evidence of many fights, both with other bears and with men, both red and white. There where claw gouges, bullet holes, an arrow head and the tip of his friend's hunting knife embedded into its chest — the tip of the knife had caught the side of its heart. Basically,

Bear had struck it a death blow, but the creature was so huge and so strong, that it had not died immediately.

Cade led Sky out toward the river, where he jumped in, fully dressed, and washed all traces of the bear's blood and hair from himself and his clothes. He couldn't rid himself of the acrid, musky smell of the creature, though. It would take a few more baths to rid him of that.

Now he'd go and show Bear that he had killed the creature, and give him the teeth and claws for his collection. Little Bird and Pack Rat would also make good use of the pelt, he knew. He waited for his clothes to dry out some, and then jumped on Sky, heading back for the town as fast as he could. He wanted to see that Bear was doing well.

Who was he kidding? He wanted to see Little Bird again.

11

As he approached the town, he could see the small fire made by Pack Rat and Little Bird. He stopped by their camp. They were sitting on a log, eating. Pack Rat rose as he dismounted, and spoke, turning to Little Bird to translate for him. She spoke quietly back to him as Cade stood, waiting. She turned to him.

'Be-xoo-kuu says you fight like a warrior, and he is proud to have you as a friend.'

Cade smiled down at her, his heart pounding.

'I am proud to have a great warrior such as Be-xoo-kuu as a friend also. To have both of you as friends. Without you, Bear would have died. My own father died when I was a small child, Wo-xuu is my family, my father.'

Pack Rat listened as she translated,

and clasped Cade's arm, pulling him close in a huge hug and slapping him on the back. Cade reciprocated, then turned to Little Bird.

'I have something for you and Pack Rat.'

He went over to Sky and pulled off the pelt. Pack Rat lifted it and gazed up at Cade, talking away. Little Bird translated.

'He says this is a grandfather bear, very powerful. The old man was very lucky to still live, and you are very powerful to have killed it.'

'It was dying when I found it. Bear had struck the killing blow; I just put it out of its misery. And skinned the big old mother.'

Pack Rat had unrolled the pelt and spread it out. Some of the town's children had seen Cade ride in and come out to see what was going on. When they saw the huge bear skin, they gathered around it, chattering excitedly.

'I need to talk to old Bear, is he awake?'

'I think, yes, he was asking for you. I tell him you went to see the white girl.'

He smiled. 'No, I went to see her father, he is the one who is paying for Bear's treatment. I thanked him and he asked me to stay here and work for him. It's a good job, with a cabin too.'

She translated for her step-brother, who spoke to Cade. Little Bird turned to him with a deep sadness in her beautiful blue eyes, a look that turned Cade's legs to jelly.

'He asks, will you stay? To work for a man with such money will be good, you will have everything.'

'I've told him I won't be staying.'

Her face lit up. Pack Rat smiled when she told him.

'I'd miss the mountains, the rivers, the fresh air. Yes, sure, the money would be good, but I've got by well enough up to now, why do I need it? I have most everything I need. I guess I'm following in Bear's old footsteps. No, just as soon as Bear is well enough to travel, I will leave this place also.'

He went on over to the infirmary to visit Bear; he needed to talk to him. The old man was sitting up in bed, being spoon-fed by the nurse, and, judging by the look on his face, thoroughly enjoying the treatment.

'Howdo, kid,' he smiled as Cade entered. 'I've landed on my feet here, eh? Clean, soft, comfortable bed, and a pretty girl to look after my every need!'

The nurse blushed and cleared away the plates, leaving the two men alone. Cade sat on the edge of the bed.

'The animal's dead. Don't you think it's time to give it up, old man?'

Cade smiled at Bear as he opened the skin pouch, and tipped out the washed teeth and claws over the bed. Bear picked them up and examined them quietly.

'What'd I do with my life? I don't know no other way, Jed. I'd die cooped up in a house — I need the wide open spaces.'

Cade smiled; he'd just given almost the same speech to Phillips and to the

Indians, so he knew what the old man was talking about.

'I sure know what you mean, but we nearly lost you this time. If it hadn't been for Pack Rat and Little Bird — '

'Don't go gettin' sentimental on me, kid. I know I nearly didn't make it, and I know next time could be my last, if I'm out in the wild when it happens, no one near . . . ' his voice tailed off.

'Yeah, see, that's what I mean, and what will Little Bird do then?'

'She's got Pack Rat to look out for her. He's her brother, he has to.'

'Half-brother, and what about when he marries, what'll she do then?'

'Hell, kid, I can't take her off with me, can — Oh.'

His eyes shone with humor, and recognition of what Cade was trying, in a very round about way, to say.

'I see how it goes, kid. You want to take responsibility for her?'

Cade looked away from that knowing gaze, and coughed to hide his embarrassment.

'Well . . . I just reckoned she'd need someone to watch out for her. Mind you, she actually seems perfectly able to look out for herself.'

He smiled, remembering how she'd fought with the two men.

'Have you spoken to her about it?'

'Not yet, wanted to know how you'd feel?'

'How d'you feel about her, Jed, other than just 'wanting to watch out for her' I mean?'

'I — well — she makes me feel calm, Bear. She takes all that anger from out of me, eases my mind. She smells of honey, and meadow flowers in the spring, and I go weak when she smiles at me. So — I guess — I guess I must love her.'

Bear laughed out loud, then grabbed at his side with a gasp, giggling until tears rolled down his face.

'Well I guess so! I wondered how long it would take. I watched the two of you when you thought I was asleep. She feels the same way, I can tell. Go to her and tell her. Go on!'

He waved his hand toward the door. Cade leaped up and left without another word. He marched through the town and out to the small camp. The two Indians were pegging out the pelt, in preparation to strip off the flesh from the skin, the small gang of children watching every move in fascination. Pack Rat turned at his approach and Little Bird went into the tipi. Cade shooed the children away. Pack Rat stood in front of the doorway, blocking him. Cade was puzzled and tried to pass the man, who stepped in front of him. Cade looked at him questioningly, and called out.

'Little Bird, I want to talk to you. Will you come out here, please?'

Be-xoo-kuu held up his hand.

'Cade, talk, Be-xoo-kuu.'

He motioned to the log, and sat down, Cade followed suit.

'Cade, talk,' the Indian said, looking him square in the eyes, with what looked remarkably like a smile, on his usually stern features.

'Be-xoo-kuu, I would like Little Bird to come with me. I would like to care for her as you do now, in your place.'

Be-xoo-kuu stopped him, and talked fast, the hidden girl translated.

'He says you will want to live in white man's house, stay in town, not live in mountains, and forests. Little Bird would die.'

'No, no house, I live like you do, in the mountains and forests, like Bear does. Always have — I know no other way. Be-xoo-kuu, I would like Little Bird to be my wife.'

He heard a gasp from the tipi. Pack Rat smiled and spoke in his own language, and Cade heard Little Bird answer quietly. Pack Rat spoke to Cade, Little Bird whispering from within the tipi.

'Be-xoo-kuu says, he knew when you looked at me the first time that this day would come soon. He asks me what it is, I want.'

'And what do you say?' asked Cade,

feeling stupid talking to the side of a tipi.

'I say, if my father Wo-xuu, and my brother Be-xoo-kuu agree, then it is right for me to do this.'

'No, never you mind what they say, what do you say, you, yourself? What does Little Bird want? What do you say to me?'

He got up and went to the tipi, pulling aside the skin that covered the entrance. Little Bird stood there looking up at him, big blue eyes shining. Cade knew he'd never seen anything as beautiful.

'Nii-ehihi says, if you wish to keep living as you have, and not to work for the white man who saved Wo-xuu, if you live in the mountains and meadows, and not in the white man's houses, she will come with you.'

Cade's heart leaped.

'Little Bird, I love you.'

He held his arms out and she went to him. He held on to her like a drowning man and she clung to him, both trying to get as close as possible. Pack Rat looked on, arms folded, trying to appear stern, but with more than a hint of a smile on his face. He knew that this white man was a good man, and would look after his sister well.

'Little Bird think that love is how I feel for you too, Cade,' she whispered into his broad shoulder.

Then Pack Rat gently separated them and sent her back into their tipi. He was taking his brotherly responsibilities very seriously. They all hung around the town until Bear was fit to travel again, Cade picking up odd jobs here and there, and then they packed up their belongings and headed out, as a group, towards the mountains. Bear had told Cade they were heading for the nearest Arapaho village so that Cade and Little Bird could be married in their way. It was over a week away.

Meantime, Cade was to have nothing to do with Little Bird, not even speak to her, unless he needed a translator for Pack Rat and Bear wasn't around. Now, she had to remain in the custody of her brother until they were married in three weeks' time. It was, by far, the hardest thing Cade had ever had to do. To keep away from the woman he loved, and be so close every day, was the worst form of torture he could imagine. But he kept his word.

The little party made good time in reaching the Arapaho village and Cade noticed that the inhabitants made a great fuss, not only of the two Indian members of the party, but Bear was also greeted like a long lost uncle. Introductions were made, and explanations. Little Bird was whisked off by her friends, amid lots of giggling and glances at Cade, to be ensconced with the other young women.

The men crowded round Cade and Bear, admiring Sky. In their tribe, a horse with his type of markings was highly valued, and this was a particularly fine specimen, admired by all the men. Cade and Bear were escorted to the central fire where they joined with the men in passing a pipe around the circle, whilst talking about Bear's adventures, and misadventures, since last he had been with them.

They all wanted to see his latest wound, and he obliged willingly. The wound was healing well, but was still pretty angry-looking, and seeing it again, Cade wondered just how his old friend had survived that attack. It looked almost as if his whole side had been ripped out, but, though still somewhat raw, it appeared to be healing well, and Bear seemed to be pretty much back to his old self now. One or two of the men in the camp could speak passable English, and talked directly to Cade; others asked Bear to translate for them. There were many questions for them both — not a detail was spared. Bear turned to Cade, smiling peacefully.

'Y'know, Jed, they reckon they'll be singin' songs about my run-in with that devil grandfather bear for years to come! They seem to think I'm under the protection of some sort of spirit, and that the bear and the spirit fought for my life. Thank god the spirit won, eh!' he laughed.

Everyone busied themselves around the camp, doing whatever was needed, then the evening meal was prepared, and the men all sat around the fire to eat. Cade and Bear sat side by side on a large log. Bear was silent throughout the meal, despite Cade trying to draw him into a conversation. When the meal was finished. Bear sighed deeply.

'Y'know, I guess I'm getting a bit too long in the tooth for this sort of life now. I ain't never made that sort of mistake before. Next time I make a mistake it'll be my last, I know that now. It's time for me to settle somewhere.'

His voice was weak, sad. Old. He stopped, and looked off into the distance, his eyes clouding over. Cade sat patiently waiting for him to come back from wherever he'd gone. He knew this decision had to have been the hardest one the old man ever had to make in his life.

'Where'll you settle, old man? Ain't no woman'll take you on, not many other folk either. You're an ornery old coot — nobody's goin' to put up with your ways.'

'I guess I'll have words with their big Chief, my wife was his daughter. Little Bird is his granddaughter so that sort of makes us brothers. They'll most likely let me stay with them, that way I can still move around the country and do a lot of the things I've always done. There's plenty ways I can help them out — I reckon I've still got a fair few pretty useful years left in me yet.'

He absently rubbed at his side and winced. It was still painful and served to remind him of his almost fatal mistake. They remained in the camp and Cade was kept apart from Little Bird for the next three weeks, until the day of the wedding. He was happy, and fitted in well with the daily life of the tribe, helping out with many of the

245

tasks, going on hunting parties, and joining in with meals and meetings.

Sometimes he would catch glimpses of Little Bird with the other women and his heart leaped. Soon enough, they would be together.

12

For the wedding ceremony, Cade wore an Arapaho outfit of fringed leggings and a tunic, made of soft elk skin, with panels of beading and quilling. It fitted him so well, he felt it had been made for him, and when he asked, he was told that it had. The women had got his measurements by eye, and had created the outfit, and all the beading and quilling, in the three weeks he had been in their camp. First thing in the day, Bear came to him.

'Ok, kid, come on, time for your naming.'

'What?'

'You're marrying into the tribe, you're marrying the granddaughter of the Chief, you have to have a Native name first. Chief Great Horse is going to name you now, come on.'

'What are they calling me?'

'I ain't got no idea, they haven't told me. We'll soon find out.'

Cade followed him obediently to the Chief's tipi, where there was a gathering of the tribal elders seated around the small centre fire, all dressed in ceremonial robes.

When they left the tipi a couple of hours later, Crazy Man Jedediah Cade had been given the name of 'Koo-kut-eeneiht' — Spotted Horse.

That afternoon, the wedding ceremony took place, Chief Great Horse officiated; drums, rattles and flutes and members of the tribe singing and chanting made it something very special, and the feast afterwards went on well into the night. Cade and his new bride sat close together, holding on to one another tightly.

Towards the end of the feast, as the fire was dying and the stars were beginning to shine, a group of young men and women of the tribe came over to them and took them both by the hands, leading them out of the circle of the camp, into the darkness. Cade was unsure of what was going on until they rounded a large boulder, and saw a small tipi, beautifully decorated, with a small fire close to the entrance. They were taken in, and Cade looked around at all of the items that surrounded him: there were blankets and cooking pots, utensils, skins, jewellery, even a bow and arrows, and a tomahawk. All of their wedding gifts had been placed inside. To one side was a large and comfortable bed, with the skin of the big old bear laid out on top of it.

The young men and women left them then, and ran off chattering and laughing: they were alone in the tipi. Cade took Little Bird in his arms and kissed her for the first time. Her body yielded softly to his kiss. They separated, and walked over to the bed silently.

They didn't join the main camp for almost a week, during which time meals were left for them at the side of the rock, so they had all the time to themselves without the worry of having to hunt or prepare food. Cade knew he had never been so happy. Indeed, he didn't think he'd ever even been happy at all before. All of the anger he had lived with all his life had subsided.

When Little Bird and Cade re-joined the camp, they were welcomed as long lost family, and a larger tipi was made ready for them. Bear had recovered well; he was still limping and only doing light work, but being treated as a special person, which to Cade, as well as to the tribe, he was.

Bear came over to talk to them, and Cade drew his pretty little blue-eyed bride close. He was at peace, he belonged here. This was what his restless soul had been longing for. He wasn't a Crazy Man any longer; he was a married man. He looked down into Little Bird's big blue eyes.

He was a man at peace with the world at last.